Other Books By Daniel Peterson

Short novels

King of Shards

Novels

The Sunward Road

Free Body Diagram is a sequel to the acclaimed short novel

King of Shards.

FREE BODY DIAGRAM

by

Daniel Peterson

Third Edition

Printed 2014

ISBN: 978-0-9854957-4-9

To my friends,

who encouraged me after the first book.

FREE BODY DIAGRAM

Free Body Diagram

Heidi pulled her guts out. Coach exhorted the crew to do exactly that from two hundred meters away. The joke among the crews was that Coach had minored in Phys-Ed with a major in bellowing. "The Bellow" broke through the grunts, the slap of water, the squeak of stressed plastic, and only failed to pierce the sharp demands of the cox.

Heidi pulled her guts out, too concentrated in effort to remember the horrific image the phrase had engendered the first time she heard it. She couldn't even spare thought for her doubts about becoming crew in the four-X-plus. Why had she signed up for this abuse? She came to college to become an engineer and play basketball but, when a new friend mentioned a shortage in crew for the sculls, she thought, what the hell? And hell is what it turned out to be.

She could tell she wasn't breathing deeply enough because she had lost track of the competing boat in her peripheral vision, a lack of oxygen, not a spurt by the opponent. Her knees jammed tighter into her chest at the next stroke to exhaust the last dregs of worn breath and she gulped air so hard that it burned, along with the fire in her thighs, shoulders and back. Her rhythm faltered. She forced calm, caught the pace, smoothed her breathing and realized the opposing team had indeed put on a spurt. Hormone monsters, she thought. They had looked only dubiously feminine to her at the start, and Heidi couldn't imagine how a normal crew could be that much better than the amazing women in her shell.

1

She rowed number one and liked the spot. It encouraged her effort, watching the others "pulling their guts out". Rowing at four would be hard, just living on trust that the other three were giving it everything. The rest of the crew were all larger than she, despite her reputation as the big muscle on her old high-school basketball team. She liked that, too.

No, she was being mean. The other team was not packing Y chromosomes, they were just better, but, she thought, I'm all out of guts. And she could see that strain had roughened the catch of the other three women.

They did not give up, but they did not win, and this was their last chance to stay in the spring competitions.

Jordan J. Winslow's early August arrival on campus went unheralded, which suited him well; he was a private person who neither expected nor wanted heraldry. Jordan, or Joe, or JJ, or Jord, or Winnie to his friends, depending on which friend (one acquaintance called him Jor, pronounced Hor, until he objected), arrived four weeks before term began. This gave him two weeks until the first faculty meeting so he could wander around exploring the S. U. campus and the small town of Evansville abutting it.

He had been shaken when Boeing laid him off (and three-hundred-twenty-two others) at the end of the last contract with Nippon Air. Eight years of dedicated work didn't guarantee continued employment. At least he had put aside some money and acquired his Professional Engineer's license before the ax fell. Other jobs were not forthcoming, in fact were damned scarce, despite his history. Everybody wanted five years experience in HVAC—not his specialty. When the recession hit he changed tack and decided to get his master's degree. State University had accepted him (and his proposed thesis developing

2

a better algorithm to predict fatigue failure in combined composite and isotropic materials), and offered him a teaching assistant position to defray costs.

"What?" he said distractedly to the stranger he discovered standing beside him.

"I said, those girls really give it a hundred and ten percent."

"Women. In college they're women, barring the occasional genius from middle school. And no, they don't give it one hundred ten percent. A hundred percent is the whole package. You can't give more than you have. But a hundred—they do that."

The sculling teams were practicing and Jordan was fascinated. He had spotted the sleek craft and flashing oars during his Monday walk through Riverbend Park and could not look away. The beauty and grace, like all sports at their highest level, equaled or exceeded that of ballet. The smooth melding of human and machine made his engineer's heart lift, and he was not immune to a male admiration for the sweaty exertion of these magnificent young women.

He turned to look at the dumpy man beside him and said, "I prefer women to girls. How 'bout you?"

The stranger blushed, muttered a quiet curse and slumped away across the park.

Jordan found a picnic table in the shade of a maple and stood on it to get a better view. He watched for two hours until the coach, audible even here, commanded the crews to break off and shower. He jumped down and trotted toward the dock while the women, in another precise maneuver, hoisted the shell from the water, over their heads, then down on one hip, and marched it to the boat shed.

By the time he got there they had all gone except for the coach who was wiping the overturned hull with a soft cloth. He stood peering into the dark through the open double door of the shed. He said, "Excuse me."

Catherine Sinjohn, aka Coach, squinted at the silhouette framed against the August afternoon light. It was slim and tall, around her own six foot two inch height. She saw a hint of closely trimmed beard, glasses, careless hair, and ears that would be comfortable on a sock monkey.

"Yes?"

Jordan stepped two paces in. "I was watching practice. This boat is great. Can I have a look?"

Catherine, tall, slim, muscular and thirty-four years old, knew men, and she knew their clumsy routines. This approach would not get beyond a good look at the shell; she wasn't in a mood to play the game and already had an adequate boyfriend. Not that she should judge men too harshly. Her height and her vibrant red hair fought to dominate the attention of admirers, which included every heterosexual man in line-of-sight. Though bored by the predictability of men, she was usually a risk-taker, able to order beer in three languages but only ask where the toilet was in one. She claimed her ancestors had been Vikings, and nobody had the temerity to refute it.

"Sure," she said.

Jordan's eyes took time adjusting to the gloom, so he used his hands, gently stroking the smooth curves, carefully testing the flex of the delicate oar riggers, lightly rapping the hull and pressing on it to test thickness and resilience, checking the rigidity in the gunwale with a torsional grip, lifting at the bow to weigh the boat. Then he could see better. He squatted below the cradle to look up to the interior at the seat glides and bulkheads.

Catherine smiled to herself and thought, he actually wanted to see the boat.

"Fiberglass," Jordan said. "Why not carbon-fiber?"

"Can't afford it."

He looked up when she answered and he finally saw her whole presence. His eyes blinked rapidly, unstoppable, a nervous affliction he suffered only when under scrutiny from a beautiful woman. Jordan's imagination flashed through a chain of possible life circumstances that could have directed this woman to become an educator instead of a fashion model.

"Ah, w-w-well," he stuttered. Oh shit, he said to himself. "Th-th-thanks."

He stood, caught himself in the beginning of a Mr. Hulot bow, straightened and walked out the door.

Catherine chuckled and shook her head.

Afternoons and evenings Jordan tried the bistros and restaurants, usually capping his day with a drink or two at one of the bars. They were practically empty this far ahead of term, even on weekends.

Two establishments had potential. One, The Arboretum, was all hardwood and heavy oak furniture, with an independent eatery through one door from which you could order good basic food. The nacho plate was heaven. An attached, glittery, intimate little wine bar was visible through a second door.

The other place was the frayed looking VFW lodge, where they asked you to sign the guest register for obscure legal reasons. The drinks were cheap and they had a small stage with a big dance floor. A friendly server explained that, when term began, they would have live music Thursday through Saturday every week. She did not know why the place was called the Topping Bar.

When the sculling teams practiced he took a Thermos of strong green tea, crackers, cheese, an apple and binoculars to the river, parking himself at the picnic table under the maple.

Jordan spent most of his official two weeks before classes developing a lesson plan with the help of his adviser, while working through the textbook he would use to teach dynamics in general engineering. He was shocked at how much he had forgotten. In the industry he had used a narrow range of principles that applied to his daily work, and relied heavily, with complete faith, on computer software generated by other engineers. Getting back to an understanding of engineering basics and, worse, trying to explain it to college sophomores, would be a challenge.

On his adviser's suggestion he introduced himself to a couple of other engineering TAs to form a small cooperative of mutually supportive teachers. If one couldn't take a class, somebody else would fill in on short notice. They were both men, twenty three and twenty four years old, also working on their masters and seeming very young to him. Jordan, at thirty three, was the old man. They were satisfyingly impressed by his eight years in industry and his PE license. Their names were James DeWitt and, the younger man, David Chan.

Friday, a week before term opened, they invited him out drinking. Jordan had gone through and out of his heavy alcoholic phase during college, but he didn't refuse the occasional excess for celebrations. James told him that faculty commonly cut loose just before the students flocked into town. More discretion would be expected afterward to maintain what little respect they could.

6

Free Body Diagram

The sign read Crustacean Chalk Circle. "Why is it called that?" Jordan asked, gesturing up as they walked under it.

"Don't know," David said. "Might have to do with the chalk for the cue-sticks and the shrimp basket they specialize in."

"So it's a pool hall? Been a while since I shot pool."

James said, "We're not here to hustle money, just fun."

James put his name on the waiting list for a pool table and they settled onto bar stools. One leisurely drink later they hit the top of the list and began a rotating series of games of eight-ball. Two would play, one would watch. They were still getting acquainted so conversation was intermittent and general, but became more amiable and revealing with every drink.

Jordan learned that David was married but waiting on his wife's arrival from Pullman while she shut down the leased apartment and spent her last two weeks at the job she was leaving to follow him.

James had partied too heavily in earlier semesters and stood a year behind on the track his parents dreamed of. The fiscal faucet had been screwed down as a result. He was between personal commitments but already had his eye on a buxom, fellow TA.

Reluctantly, Jordan told them of his regretful marriage as a college junior to a woman who had seemed strong and self confident, but turned out to be pig-headed and self important, with a huge sense of entitlement. Pretty much an Evil Princess of the old school. Before graduation he had traveled to three job interviews. At the third, he received a text from his wife explaining that she was not willing to follow him around the country when she already had a life, and, incidentally, she had screwed the roommate as soon as Jord left for the first interview.

7

Jordan had become gun-shy, hooked up a few times when hormones demanded, but avoided commitment.

"By text!" James said. "That's cold."

Around ten thirty a subtle lull in the din caught their attention. They watched the cause of it walk along the bar and step up to an empty stool beside an athletic man. Jordan recognized the sculling coach. She wore khaki hiking shorts, sand colored sandals and a sky blue tank-top over a purple sport bra. Her flame of hair reclined in a broad French braid.

"Holy shit," Jordan said.

James turned a smile on him and said, "Give it up. That's a ball buster."

"She seemed OK the other day."

"You met her? And lived?"

"No," Jord said sarcastically. "She killed me with a single blow from her delicate right fist. *You* don't know her."

"True. But I've heard rumors."

"What's her name?"

"He's doomed," David said. "Just shoot him now."

"Catherine," James said. "Don't call her Cathy."

The room full of students intimidated him despite the ease he had achieved in meetings and presentations at Boeing. The chime sounded. He took a blank sheet of lined paper to the nearest student.

"Please write your name and pass it back."

Seat shuffling, paper sliding and murmurs accompanied the attendance sheet around the room. Jordan studied each student, placing them in a mental map so he could connect faces

8

with names. He frowned when he saw the third student back in the middle. She looked very familiar.

Right! She rows in the sculls, at the bow position. He remembered her lean strength, and now he made note of her velvet skin the color of creamed coffee, a close aura of black, rippled hair and an oval face. Her dark, serious eyes followed the progress of the attendance sheet. He judged her looks at around seven on the scale and felt a twinge of guilt for having rated her.

The sheet made it to the last desk where Jordan timed his arrival to match. He walked slowly back to his lectern, scanning the names and counting. Heidi van Vleet. Jordan smiled. Names were not predictors of geographical origin.

That was not true in her case. Heidi's mixed-race grandparents had toughed it out as long as they could in apartheid South Africa. Such couples were harassed, or disappeared, or murdered. He, descended from Boers and fifteen years older than his dark wife, was an established doctor so they had enough status to delay the inevitable and, better, the money to emigrate. They settled in Minneapolis because they had never heard of it, except to know that it was not in the southern United States where they feared the KKK would pick up the torch of apartheid.

The surrounding neighbors in the middle-class suburb looked a lot like her, on average, by the time she was born. New couples of dramatically different skin color were still settling there because of her pioneering grandparents and others like them. Disparity from the norm becomes the norm if it is common enough. She once thought, when her father was teaching her to play chess, that she could pick sixteen random people in the nearest three blocks and have a complete set of game pieces.

Jordan developed an urge that, three weeks into the term, made him invite Dave and Jim to the pool hall, but Dave's wife had arrived, and Jim was entertaining his plush TA.

He let another week slide and tried again. They were still busy, so he went solo.

He sat at the bar, nursing a screwdriver. The phrase struck him after the third drink—nursing a screwdriver. Maybe, he thought, I should be milking a White Russian. He absently watched the closest pool game, attuned to the potential shift in attention that would mark the arrival of Catherine. His fourth drink was half gone when he felt the crowd focus on the door. He casually turned to look. A man, at least six foot four, broad shouldered, slim, confident and slow, strolled past.

Jordan sighed, tossed back the rest of his drink, checked his pile of change lying in a puddle on the bar, added a dollar bill to it, and left.

Jordan's next three weeks were filled by struggles with his own master-level courses, searching thesis related literature of best practices, outlining preliminary experiments for his thesis, and assisting his mentor in the professor's research.

Knuckles rapped at the jam of the always-open door to his cupboard-sized office. Heidi stood in the gap with a pack slung on one shoulder and her hips shifted for balance.

"Yes!" Jord said, more enthusiastically than intended. "What's up?"

She smiled nervously, "I'm not getting it."

"Getting what?"

"Dynamics doesn't make sense."

"We can handle that. Sit."

She settled in the chair, dropping her pack on the floor. "I'm really trying to follow, but it's like a foreign language. And I have time issues. Worn out by nine at night. Can't put in late hours without passing out."

"The rowing," he said.

Her eyebrows raised, she made the connection, grinned and blurted, "You're the one..." She stopped.

"That watches practice."

"Sorry. We thought it was some creep."

Jord laughed. "Who knows? But your problem. You could study with a classmate."

"Blind leading the blind?"

He shrugged. "Okay. I can set you up with an upper-level, student tutor. If you can stay awake. Doesn't cost much."

Her family, descended from strong roots, had great expectations for her. The parents covered her expenses, but demanded to know where every penny went. She couldn't hide the cost of a tutor or answer their accusing questions about why she needed one.

"I hoped you could coach me."

The word "coach" galvanized him.

He frowned in thought about the heavy schedule he faced, the demands of his busy professor, and the papers lying uncorrected in his desk drawer. He thought about spending time with this attractive young woman who could not, in any moral or ethical way, be thought of as an attractive young woman. Future pathways blossomed and branched in his mind and he imagined Catherine, the sculling coach, slowly walking the length of the

Crustacean Chalk Circle to park herself on the bar stool next to him and lean against his shoulder.

"Okay," he said. "Jot down your schedule, post it to me, and I'll get back to you about when we can work."

"Thanks." She smiled and stood. "And sorry about the 'creep' thing."

"No problem. I try not to make it a practice, but men in general *are* creeps."

She laughed, shouldered her pack and left.

Two days later Jordan found Heidi's neat spreadsheet in his messages and realized that she had taken him too literally about her schedule. He printed a copy. He had expected a short list of available times, but everything was there, including morning rising and shutting off the light at night. A small block of time was left open each evening which would otherwise be earmarked for a meager social life. He uncapped a pen and crossed those out. He scratched jagged lines through the weekend. There was a free hour before afternoon sculling practice, three days of the week, just following dynamics class. That would be convenient for them both. One hour a week should be enough, and Monday was his preference. If more was needed, she could opt in for the other two hours, though he hoped she would avoid Friday.

They had two things in common. One thing was being addressed by the tutoring. The other was a tall, Nordic, red-haired woman whom they both wanted to please. The first occupied more of the hour, but the second intruded during social amenities at the beginning and end in discussions of sculling.

"So, you didn't do well last year?" Jordan asked at the end of a session.

"No. And not for the seven years before I got here."

"How long has Ca...Coach been here?"

"About four years, I guess. And she's good. Can't blame her. Or the teams."

"So," Jordan said. "That only leaves two possibilities: bad luck, or bad equipment."

Heidi nodded. "It *is* an old boat."

"I noticed. Not even carbon fiber."

They sat thinking about the implications for a moment, then Heidi shrugged. "Nothing we can do about that or the luck."

She stuffed her things into the backpack and stood. "See you later."

Jordan gave her an absent nod and smile, then sat staring out the window. She's right about the luck, he thought, but not about the equipment. He stared vacantly for eight minutes, until a smile crinkled his eyes.

"Wait, wait," Mr. Montaigne, the dean of engineering said. "You want to take over the junior M. E. lab project?"

"Not take it over," Jordan replied. "Just suggest a project, and assist with it."

"Why?"

"It's related to my thesis."

"Not a compelling reason—replacing the original project just to help you. Can you give me something else?"

"How about a winning sculling team?"

Professor John Durning ME, PE, PhD, was pissed-off at the late change in his lab's project, for both logistical and personal reasons. He had already primed the students and got them brainstorming on his plan for an after-market hybrid attachment for existing cars, a potentially patentable, marketable and reputation building device. Now here was this young, asshole TA going over his head and usurping his course by massaging the dean's addiction to school sports. And girl sports! Title IX crap!

It didn't help that Durning knew he'd look like an idiot trying to direct a project based on composite materials and fluid flow. Talk power trains and energy storage and he was at the cutting edge, but he hadn't kept up on structural materials.

"A boat," Durning muttered. "A goddamn boat with no commercial value."

"What?" Jordan asked.

"A goddamn boat! The world is begging for solutions to climate change and we build a boat for a handful of girls."

"Women."

Durning glared at Jordan. I knew it, he said to himself.

"And," Jordan said, "the technology relates directly to saving energy by vehicle weight reduction."

"Then let's put it on a real vehicle instead of a floating splinter."

"Problem is, the boat itself will be overwhelming. No way we could work up a drive-train in the time we have."

Durning grumbled under his breath again.

Jordan looked expectant.

Durning said, "Yes. I know. So we better take the class down to the boat shed and get a base reference."

"Exactly," Jordan agreed. "I'll make an appointment with the coach." He turned away, hoping that Durning hadn't noticed the rise of color to his face.

Jordan wasn't sure what was happening to him. Since his disastrous marriage to The Demon Princess he had been almost indifferent to women, not immune but disinterested. What was special about this admittedly beautiful, confident, tall, muscular woman? Time, he thought, really does heal, even if it's hard to believe during the long grief.

Catherine's office phone number was in the university's web directory in the athletics department. Luckily she was the only Catherine so now he also knew her last name, and, in the secure pages of the web site, he could locate her cell-phone number, just in case.

She had not answered the messages left on her office phone even by three o'clock the next afternoon. He resorted to the cell number and got voice-mail. Wednesday, still lacking a response, Jordan gestured Heidi over as she came into the classroom.

"Could you see me after class?"

"Sure. What's up?"

"I need to get in touch with your sculling coach."

She gave him a smile that he chose not to interpret, nodded and went to her desk.

Twenty minutes of The Magnificent Seven had played when Jordan's cell phone toned the notes of Beethoven's Ode to Joy: Catherine's number. He set aside the rum-and-coke, stopped the video (he usually just watched the beginning anyway) and took the call.

"Hello."

"Heidi says you want to talk to me. Something about turning our luck around, a winning season."

He breathed slowly. "Yes. I noticed that your shell is old technology. I have an idea to change that."

"Noticed? When...? Oh! I know you. I never put it together when Heidi said her dynamics teacher was the 'Watcher'. You're the guy that stroked the boat like a lost lover."

There was that heat in his face again. Dammit! How does she do this to me?

"That's me."

"What's the deal?"

"I persuaded the engineering dean to build you a boat in the junior ME lab project. The beauty is, it's already budgeted. If we need more money he's willing to help, and even believes the Engineering Excellence Grant could be tapped."

"You're kidding."

"Dead serious."

The pause went for ten seconds. "What will it take?"

"First, we need to get the lab students into your boat-shed to see what you have. Then we'll have to take some video of it in action. Then we need to get your input so we don't make ignorant assumptions. Then," he hesitated, "you need to have a drink with me at the Crustacean Chalk Circle tomorrow."

This pause lasted only two seconds. "You're a pushy bastard." She chuckled.

Jordan piled all of his hope upon that chuckle.

"No," she continued, "I have other things going tomorrow night. But be in my office at eight in the morning so you can fill me in. Room 324 in the Whole Health building. See you then."

The connection died. He began to live.

He arrived at precisely eight and tapped lightly at the open office door.

She hammered intently on the keyboard, frowning at the screen. "Come on," she said with a quick glance. "Sit down. Just a moment."

Catherine's face relaxed into a semi-smile and she drew back from the keyboard, swept the mouse across the pad and clicked. "Gone," she said. "If you don't keep up with at least the official crap, it buries you."

She raised her eyebrows and gestured toward the coffee dripper. "Coffee?"

"Sure. Thanks" He had been fine until she held his gaze, then the old affliction fluttered his eyes until he turned to study her office, the hazardously arrayed equipment, the stacked books and the dramatic posters exhibiting supreme athletic efforts.

Filling a paper cup plucked from an inverted stack, she studied him. Not a bad looking guy, though not classically handsome, and obviously not overly confident. She slipped a fuzzy insulating cone onto the cup and passed it over.

Jordan avoided her eyes by studying the steaming cup and blowing on its surface.

"Cream? Sugar?" she asked.

"No, thanks." He sipped, burnt his lip, grimaced and finally looked at her.

"So you're going to build us a super-shell and we'll take all the trophies," she said.

"That's the plan."

"Why?"

Jordan looked perplexed. "What do you mean, 'Why'?"

"Just out of the blue you decide we're a charity case that deserves your beneficence, or is it just about that drink you wanted to share tonight?"

He laughed. "Actually, it's related to my master's degree. The data we generate will be crucial to the mathematical model I'm working on. Though, to be honest, I hope you'll give me a rain-check on that drink."

She gave him a dubious look. "What makes this boat so great?"

"It'll be state-of-the art. Feather-light but stronger than alloy steel. This is what I worked on at Boeing."

After a moment's thought she said, "That would be good. You realize, though, that below a specific weight, that doesn't help? We'd have to add weight to compete, by the rules."

"I didn't know, but that's why we have to consult with you and your teams. And, wait a minute." He unfocused while ramifications paraded through his mind. "Is it required that the extra weight go in the shell, or maybe move with the rowers?"

"With that heavy dinosaur we row, I never had to find out."

"OK. Then minimizing the weight is still best as long as we put the handicap weight near as possible to the center-of-mass of each rower. They won't have to work at accelerating separated masses toward and away from each other. If the crew was just springs, it wouldn't matter, but people aren't springs."

"What are you talking about?"

Now he smiled with confidence. "Let me draw you a sketch. This is called a free body diagram. We represent a dynamic system in its simplest form and eliminate all influences that don't address the question..."

The project started moving forward quickly once the students became excited by the challenge and understood some of the difficulties. Jordan gave them direction for researching composite laminating technology and suggested experiments. They ran the sculling shell through a hard practice session, laden with strain gauges and recorded by six cameras, all the data synchronized and fed to the computer on a pilot boat. They held brainstorming meetings and came up with several possible enhancements beyond the simple use of lighter material, including mounting the seats solid and putting the oar riggers on slides, hull chines to flatten the wake and recover it's energy, an underwater bow point to emulate the bulb on ocean liner hulls, and, this from Professor Durning, bungee cords on the seats to store the energy of sliding forward between stokes to return it *during* strokes. A professor teaching fluid mechanics heard of the project and volunteered help in the fluid studies. They worked on an idea Jordan had for a lighter, stronger lamination core.

Jordan suggested Heidi find a little time to work with the lab students on motion studies to give her a real-world feel for dynamics.

Heidi, struggling to tie together a disparate and demanding schedule, left the noisy apartment that she shared with Lisa and Melanie, basketball players that she'd known before she went to rowing, and carried her full pack of books and homework to the Student Union Building. She settled into the lounge with a veggie hoagie and a milkshake. Applying oneself is the mantra, but not the panacea. She drudged at her stack of work.

A man's hand set a medium diet cola into one small empty spot among her spread of papers and texts. She followed the muscular arm up along the body to the face while taking an increasingly deep breath.

"I saw you here when I came through two hours ago, and you're still here. Time for a break. Have a drink and visit."

She thought, oh my God. He was six three, two hundred forty pounds, without a hint of fat. And he had a nice, dimpled smile.

Two busy weeks and everything in Jordan's projects were coming smoothly together. Then Heidi van Vleet missed Monday class, practice, and lab. She missed Wednesday. She had given Jordan her cell number when he began tutoring her, so Thursday evening he called. It went straight to voice mail. When she missed Friday, Jordan called Catherine.

"Do you know what's going on with Heidi?" he asked.

A long pause held the line. "Well," Catherine said and the pause continued. Just before Jordan asked if she was still there, Catherine said, "She has personal problems. We're hoping to take care of it this weekend. She might be in class Monday. I hope she hasn't missed anything important."

"Nothing we can't pick up in tutoring."

"She won't make it to tutoring for a while. And the boat lab is out, too."

"That doesn't sound good. Can I help?"

Free Body Diagram

"No. We'll handle it."

Gerard "Grid" Deimos, star tackle of the university's mediocre football team but angry at the world because his lamp lay under the peck basket of the only third-rate school that would give him a scholarship, took his usual shortcut across the track field. The field was very dark but familiar, and he could guide toward the distinctive lights of his frat house. He was at no risk of harm. Few who saw his impressive height, breadth and definition would consider him an easy target, and nobody who knew him would risk his perpetual, unpredictable rage. He had received warnings for a couple of hushed-up incidents involving alcohol and broken bones, others' bones, not his.

A fair amount of alcohol pumped in his veins at the moment and, though his Saturday visit to the bar had not caused injuries, nobody from his frat house chose to accompany him. He walked alone.

Five barely visible figures coalesced around him. Taser darts spiked his back and he dropped to his knees twitching, then fell face forward. His hands and ankles were gathered and cinched in zip-ties. After a pause for the return of mental clarity, as much as was available to him, a female voice said, "We know you have brutalized women. We know that you will never do it again. Can you hear me?"

"Goddamn fucking bitch!" he bellowed. "I'll rip your fucking head off!"

A club, made of one inch galvanized pipe padded in pipe insulation and duct tape, slammed against the side of his skull.

He paused for a breath and roared every insult and threat that he could dredge up. Blows from clubs rained down hard all over his body until shock overwhelmed his adrenalin and he lay puffing short, rapid breaths.

"You will never rape another woman."

Grid shrieked in frustrated rage and a club caught him in the jaw, shutting it off. His cut tongue poured blood.

"You will never beat another woman."

He was a slow learner but began to get the message. So he just lay puffing in fury.

"The reason you will never assault another woman is that this is not the worst that can happen to you. You are just beginning to understand the humiliation, helplessness and fear in your victims. We'll ratchet that up."

The clubs went to work with method, raising bruises all over, breaking one forearm, a collar bone, and fracturing his left cheek bone. He began to wail again but shut it off as consciousness faded. They stopped.

He returned and slurred, "What."

"Good. Now you're listening. Repeat after me. You will NEVER brutalize another woman."

"I will never brutalize another woman."

"Say it again."

"I will NEVER brutalize another woman."

"Good," she said. And he felt the ordeal was ending. Then his pants were stripped off and seven inches of a rough broom-handle were forced into his rectum.

He shrieked and a club shut him up.

Now he was crying.

"Can you hear me?" the voice asked.

"Yes," he sobbed.

"This is what your victims feel. This is what you do to them. Not fun, is it?"

He just blubbered.

"IS IT!"

"NO! No. No."

"Now THIS is why you will never assault another woman. Next time, we will take all of your equipment. Cock, balls, the works. You'll squat to piss the rest of your miserable life. Will you ever assault another woman?"

"No," he moaned. "No. No. Never."

Wire-cutters flashed in the dim light from large Greek letters. The zip-ties were cut apart and removed. The broom handle was not.

Heidi appeared in class. Jordan was pleased to see her but noticed she looked different. Her manner varied between closed isolation and forced ebullience. She was brittle. She would not meet his eye during class and ignored his attempts to get her attention, even his calling her name, after class. She did not wear her book-pack on her shoulder, but held it to her chest in tightly crossed arms beneath her tucked chin, and scurried out of the classroom.

On Tuesday the lab students collected the laser mapper that the art and architecture college was loaning them. They set it up on the pad outside the sculling boat shed and carried the rowing shell out to prop carefully, hull up, about fifteen meters away in front of the laser head. The three dimensional scan of one half of the shell was stored in the laptop hard drive. They rolled the boat over gently, under the watchful eye of Coach Catherine, readjusted the padded supports, jacked the laser two meters higher and scanned the top-side. Wielding tape measures, squares, levels and notepads the students made detailed sketches of the interior and the simple mechanical parts of the boat. They measured the oars, weighed them and noted the details of the oarlocks.

Back at the lab the three dimensional computer model of the half-shell was converted to a CAD file and mirrored to form a full hull. For two days they added interior structural details. Thursday evening three students who really had the fire in their bellies began sketching the improvements that had come up during brainstorming.

Friday afternoon Jordan thumbed through a small stack of prints that the excited lab group had generated. It was too early to go into this much detail, but he wasn't going to discourage them.

He picked up the phone and hit the speed-dial for Catherine's number. Since they were working together she was more likely to respond to his caller-ID.

"Yes," she said.

"I have preliminary drawings to show you and get your input. How about over dinner tonight?"

"Not tonight. Me and Tony are celebrating his new job." Tony was her bronzed, muscled boyfriend.

"Oh! Great! What did he find?"

"He's got a ski instructor gig at Vail for the winter."

Jordan's heart made a little bounce. "Well," he said calmly, "that's good news. Maybe I could show you the drawings over lunch tomorrow?"

There was a brief, thoughtful pause. "Okay," she said. "Eleven thirty at The Arboretum. Dutch."

So she wants to keep it professional, Jordan thought. I'll just be persistent, stay nearby and do everything possible to avoid the potential relationship's "death by friendship". Do NOT let her start thinking of us as friends. Keep your intentions obvious, but don't push too hard.

"Okay," Jordan said. "See you then."

Jordan was explaining the stationary seats with slide mounted oar riggers when Catherine interrupted.

"Nope," she said. "That puts it in the 'experimental' class. We don't want to run in that class; too few competitors to get good races. In fact these other changes might do the same thing. You can do whatever you want in hull design and weight reduction, but the judges cast a hairy eye on mechanical changes. We'd have to get a ruling before racing to make sure we don't get booted from the course."

"I'll have the students keep that in mind and make any dubious changes removable. Like the bungee cords. Simple matter of unhooking them and pulling them out."

Catherine scooped the last of the guacamole with a nacho chip. "Fine. Is that all?" She crunched the nacho.

"For now. We'll get together about other changes. Thanks for the insight."

"Sure. By the way, the weather's looking like we can get in a practice this afternoon. In case you want to perch on your picnic table for the show." She smiled.

"Thanks. I will," he said with the chagrin she had hoped for.

Jordan had downloaded the rules for competition rowing just after the dean accepted his proposal. He knew that the sliding riggers would put them out of the general class, and, though the wording was ambiguous, he thought they would not be allowed to mount the handicap weights on the rowers' seats. However, since Catherine's presence could not be replaced by a rule book, he would keep consulting her.

Catherine considered getting a copy of the rules for Jordan to reduce her work load. She didn't. It was good to be involved in the design of the new boat. And she hoped to use the crossover with engineering to help bring Heidi back out of her isolation.

The crew was Heidi's crew, but she was not in the shell. Another teammate rowed at number one. Jordan looked around until he spotted a familiar lone figure sitting on a log barrier of the hiking trail beside the river. Heidi watched the sleek craft slice through the water. Jordan gathered his gear and walked down the slope. When he sat on the log near her she turned with a start, then recognized him and again followed the boat.

He opened his pack and set out supplies between them. He uncrinkled the cracker packet and rolled back the wax on the cheese loaf. "Cheese and cracker?"

Heidi shook her head.

"It's Wensleydale."

No response.

He held up the Thermos. "Green tea?"

She shook her head.

More minutes passed uncomfortably. He said, "I hear Coach's boyfriend got a job. You know him?"

"Not really."

"They seem very different, Coach and Tony."

Heidi loosened up a bit at that remark and gave him that knowing, semi-smile look from the corner of her eye.

"Am I really that obvious?" Jordan asked.

"You might as well wear a sign."

"She's an appealing woman."

Heidi didn't answer.

They watched the boat slow at the end of the run while the exhausted crew bent over the oars and gasped for air.

"At least my position is the easiest to fill," Heidi sighed.

It was not his place, but he ached to ask what had changed her. What was the "personal problem"? How could he help? But it was not his place.

"The crew doesn't row as well without you," he said.

For a moment she was quiet. She leaned her head forward onto her arms, onto her knees and cried. In wailing sobs she cried, "He beat me! He raped me!"

"Oh God," Jordan breathed, stunned. "Oh, God." He wanted to reassure her, to hold her, to pat her, to protect her after-the-fact and prove that not all men were monsters, but knew that it would be wrong.

When she had quieted some he asked, "Did you..."

She sat up and grated out, "NO! I did NOT go to the police! I did NOT report it! I did NOT go to the hospital!" She put her face in her hands, resting her elbows on her knees. Tears crept down her forearms. "I hurt, and I was dazed. And filthy. I don't know how I got home. Took pain killers. Washed ... everything. Then I showered until the water went cold. Laid in bed and stared at the ceiling 'til sunrise. My roommates figured I was recovering from a good time." She snorted a gallows laugh. "So they left me alone until noon. They told me to report it. Everybody tells me to report it! I'm sick of it! Sick of the pushing. I just want quiet! To be left alone!"

Jordan was way out of his depth. So he did nothing but sit rigidly and look at the far shore.

The scullers returned to the dock and debarked to let the next team board. Coach took the time to look around at the uncharacteristically fine day and recognized the distant pair edgily posed on the log up the trail. She started furiously toward them intending to kick some Winslow butt. Then Heidi raised her wet face out of her hands, gave a shuddering sigh, and glanced at Jordan. She wiped her face and gazed, like him, at the other shore. She smoothed her expression. Jordan pulled a cracker out of the packet, placed a small slice of cheese onto it and set it on Heidi's knee. Coach stopped. What the hell? Heidi picked up the cracker and ate it. Coach studied them for a moment and turned back to her crews.

Brainstorming is fun. The sky is the limit, or not, and there is no box to think outside of, no boundaries at all. The students laughed frequently but uncritically. One of the best laughs came at the suggestion to emulate humpback whale fin-lumps on the oars. Then the laughter paused. Why not? They put it on the list of tests for fluid flow, including the stabilizing fin.

Jordan's idea for a light-weight lamination core had to be modified because the ideal solution involved technology that did not exist. The optional solution was to take commercial hex-core material, dip-mask the outer edges and then etch away most of the thickness in the honeycomb cell walls. This could be done in a shallow tray easily built in the ME lab so they settled for that.

Heidi called Jordan and asked if he would catch her up on dynamics with new tutor sessions. She re-joined the lab students for motion studies. She began rowing. The crew took it easy on her at first to let her get the conditioning back.

Catherine dropped in unexpectedly at Jordan's tiny office.

"You almost got your ass kicked," she said.

"What? When? Why?"

"When I saw you annoying Heidi by the river. But I guess she trusts you. So your ass will remain un-kicked for now."

"Great. Thanks. But, now you bring it up, how am I supposed to act with her?"

"For God's sake, just act like you used to. Respect her privacy. But don't treat her like a cripple. And don't treat her like a guy. The tutoring has an edge of sex, right? Don't let that edge go away. I'm not saying flirt with her, but she doesn't need to think she's damaged goods, she needs to sense a normal male heat."

Jordan blushed and had to look down at his desk to hide his damned eye-flutters. "If I can pull that off, I should get an Oscar. I can't un-know her situation."

"Okay. Then just think of it like a broken arm. The cast is there and the break will heal. But you don't have to look at it. Look at her eyes."

Jordan imagined Heidi's deep brown eyes. Yes, they are nice. He shook his head. "Okay. I get it. Please don't kick my ass if I slip now-and-then."

Catherine smiled and said, "Everybody gets a little slack."

She turned to leave and stopped. "Hey, we're giving Tony a going-away party on Saturday, two weeks from this weekend. He has to leave the week after to be in Vail to prep for the Thanksgiving Day opening. You're invited."

"Where?"

"My place."

"Where's your place?"

She picked up a pencil from his desk and jotted the address on a sticky-pad. She added date and time.

Jim called him Tuesday evening, sounding like death was knocking at his door, and asked Jordan to cover his calculus class Wednesday at ten. "Sure, what section?"

"The lesson plan is on my site," he wheezed.

"Okay. No problem."

He ran into Dave after calculus class.

"Jord!" Dave said. "I been thinking about you. You never met Debra, my wife."

"Not yet."

"We're headed to the Topping Bar tomorrow night for some dancing. Come with us."

"Uh. Three is an awkward number."

Dave looked as if he wanted to be embarrassed but couldn't quite manage. "Well, as it happens, her sister's in town for a visit. So there'd be four."

Oh God, Jordan thought, barely restraining a shudder. A blind date. And he didn't dance. "Shit, Dave. I have papers, research, the boat project, a student to tutor. I just can't make it."

"Oh, come on! A break will increase your efficiency, get that crap cleared out faster. Besides, my sister-in-law is gorgeous. You'll kick yourself if you don't go."

Life is just loaded with the unexpected. But, gorgeous or not, dancing or not, Dave was right about needing a break. "Okay. Pick me up."

Dave had not lied. Bonnie was gorgeous, twenty nine years old, blond, too well formed, and almost as smart as an appointed committee of igneous rocks. She had somehow (Jordan held an unflattering theory) worked her way into lower management at a large K-Mart store. She made reasonably good money and had been at the cliff edge of job loss when the recession-driven layoffs ended. Her estranged husband was watching the twins so she could travel to see how her Little-Sis was doing. Predatory hunger lurked in every glance she gave him.

The four of them settled into a pitcher of beer and made smalltalk during the band's first break. The musicians returned to the little stage, launched into Rock Around the Clock, and Bonnie looked at him expectantly. When she understood that he wouldn't do the asking, she did.

"I don't dance!" he yelled into her ear.

"They don't either!" she shouted back, gesturing at the flailing dancers.

She had a good point. The main qualification for dance was an ability to ignore the bad opinion of others. He shrugged and put out a hand.

She beamed, accepted the hand and joined him in aimless gyrations among the growing mass of other aimless gyrators. He noticed two or three couples who demonstrated a refined pattern in their motions, more likely from practice than chance. I guess, he thought, if you're going to spend time drinking in a place like this you might as well develop a skill. Odd that it had never occurred to him in his college drinking days.

They ordered another pitcher and let their sweat subside through the next song. Bonnie was rested and ready for the following number. Jordan smiled stiffly and found a spot with her on the crowded floor. At one point his gaze, which looked everywhere except at his partner's aggressive breasts, noticed that the dance floor was stainless steel. "Cool," he said.

They stayed on the floor for the next two songs and sat one out to cool off and replenish fluids. This drained the pitcher. Motivated by the inattention of servers, excess attention from his date and his inborn generosity, Jordan offered to order a pitcher at the bar. Besides, he was actually beginning to relax and forget the demands of daily life. And, dim or not, Bonnie was both physically stunning and suggestively interested in him. Another few beers. Just a few. It's not like he expected pillow-talk to scintillate even at the best of times and it had been a long time since *any* kind of pillow-talk.

Jordan finally caught the attention of a bartender and was ordering the beer when he was hip-bumped by somebody wedging to the bar. He finished shouting his request to the bartender while shifting to his left to let the newcomer in. The bartender collected a fistful of pitchers and swung them under a flowing tap.

The person for whom he'd made room hip-bumped him again so he glanced over. Catherine grinned at him. "You're a rotten dancer," she yelled in his ear.

He was drunk enough that his eyelids behaved themselves. "If I considered myself a dancer, I would agree," he shouted back.

Catherine looked over her shoulder. "She's good looking, your date."

He hoped the dim light hid his blush. "Attraction is more than just hair dye and strategic implants."

"They are VERY perky for their amazing size. Men aren't supposed to care if they're real."

"Depends on the circumstance. Her bust size is greater than her IQ."

"Poor Jordan," she laughed. She paid for a pair of drinks, picked them up, hip-bumped him once more and left.

She's drunk, he thought. Jord watched her thread through the dancers and disappear when she sat down at a distant table.

"Hey!" he shouted at the bartender. "Make that two pitchers!"

Jordan J. Winslow became conscious around three-thirty in the wee hours and got up to take that wee. Before leaving the bed he felt around behind him with dread. No warm, soft body lay there so he sighed both relief and alcohol vapors. He stood, staggered out and across to the bathroom with the aid of door frames. He stood unsteadily at the toilet and discovered a wrinkled condom still in place, ready for action, with no evidence of use.

"Well, old soldier," he muttered as he stripped it off, "you answered the call with honor, but were not asked to serve. It will be written that you were retired without discharge."

Memories of last night would eventually return to make him cringe in embarrassment, but for now he was fogged in blissful ignorance. When he crossed the hall back to his bedroom he noticed, dimly lit by a distant streetlight, a woman-shaped lump on the living room couch, under the afghan that usually draped the back. He shuddered and went on to bed.

Jordan woke again at eight-thirty to a pounding head and desert mouth. Crossing to the bathroom for medication and hydration, he glanced at the couch and saw that the occupant had vanished.

Avoiding Dave was possible for a few days, but the encounter was inevitable. A cackling laugh echoed down the hallway and Jordan knew he'd been caught. Dave trotted up to him still laughing loudly. "I *thought* you were a bit over-baked when I dropped you and Bonnie off. She's kind of pissed at you."

"She'll get over it," Jord replied.

"She told Debra you passed out before the engines were warmed up."

"I figured that's what happened. From the evidence, or lack of."

"You're not going to get another invite, and I bet she'd screw anything that can walk, talk and vote. Actually I'm setting her standards high. Voting is enough."

"*That* fills me with confidence. I don't want another invite."

"But, Jord, she's a looker!"

"Yes. Like a Ferrari without an engine." He tapped his temple.

Dave guffawed. "Yeah, I got the pick of that litter with Debra. But for a one-nighter...you're way too picky."

"Is she still in town?"

"Two more days."

"Please let me know where she might turn up, so I won't."

Dave laughed one more time. "Okay. If that's what you want. You wouldn't like to beg her forgiveness?"

"Get stuffed, Dave." Jordan smiled, shook his head and said, "See you later."

He walked away trailed by Dave's fading chuckle.

Water tank tests of the scale-model showed a very small decrease in drag using the wake-flattening chine. The computer analysis had suggested it would. Then Ibrahim, one of the lab students, recalled that the video of the existing boat showed the hull bobbing up and down several centimeters at each oar stroke. They emulated this in the model and found that the chine actually increased drag, so it was eliminated.

They had better luck with the sub-surface bow bulb. It tolerated a wide depth variation while producing good drag reduction. Ibrahim, again, noticed that the bulb seemed to accomplish the same wake flattening that they had hoped for from the chine. Jordan insisted that the students create a means of attachment for the bulb that would allow it to be removed without spoiling the smooth surface of the hull if the judges rejected it. A short brainstorming session suggested a vacuum system, essentially large suction cups, that held the parts firmly together, perfectly mated.

Catherine lived in a rented house on the east side of Evansville, where housing was cheap and the neighbors unsavory.

Jordan both dreaded and looked forward to the party. He realized that he wouldn't know anybody except the hostess. Parties at Boeing had always been with friends, some acquaintances and, at worst, like-minded social butterflies. Many of them loved sports, but none of them made their living in sports. Jordan hated sports. Well, not hated, and not all sports. He loved bicycling and hiking and cross country skiing, but to sit and watch a bunch of hormonally enhanced, short-lived specialists pound against each other was not his idea of sport, so he preferred competitions like sculling and curling and tennis, games he never had tried, and which are not considered money-making exhibitions for television. He still didn't know where to categorize golf and bowling, though surely they have to fit into the curling group. Neither interested him enough to know the top competitors. For several years he had thought that Tiger Woods was a particularly dangerous forest in the Bengal, or so he claimed.

Jordan carried a bottle of mid-quality, dry Riesling, a quart of artichoke heart dip, and two large boxes of Wheat Thins. He didn't know that there was a local semi-pro, woman's rugby team in Evansville, but the tanned woman with oak thighs who answered the door had obviously not bothered to change, or shower, since the afternoon match. She smiled when he exhibited his contribution, said, "Scrumptious,"with a grin and allowed him in. She directed him toward the refreshments to drop off his goods, where he traded them for a pint glass of home brewed beer.

Nobody looked familiar. They all looked exceedingly fit. Not that he himself looked out of place; he just *felt* out of place. He milled aimlessly for a while, slowly draining the surprisingly good glass of beer. Oh God, he thought belatedly, glancing with a smile at the stout rugby player greeting people at the door. She said scrum-chess. He spotted an unobtrusive corner to settle in but first went back for a refill. The little bit of home brew had been consumed already so he drew a glassful of Coors from the tapped keg. He reclaimed his corner but had only been there a moment when Tony, whom he knew by sight but had not met, saw him and jostled through the happy crowd to his side.

"Hi," Tony said. "I'm Tony. You must be Jordan, the boat guy."

"Hi, Tony. That's me, but I prefer 'engineer guy'." He smiled.

"Okay," Tony laughed. "How's the boat coming?"

"Should be ready for a trial run by mid February so we can have it for the first March competition."

"And it'll give our scullers the edge they need to win?"

"That's the plan. By the way, congrats on your job."

"Thanks. It should be fun, working with the tourists.

"You're a people person."

"When the people are young, female and eager to learn to ski."

Jordan glanced around the room.

Tony laughed. "No, Catherine doesn't feel threatened. We have a non-possessive relationship."

Jord raised his eyebrows. "That's modern, I guess. How did you two meet?"

"Two summers back she and a couple of her friends vacationed at the tourist ranch in Jackson Hole where I was working. The Liebe Ranch E."

Jordan suppressed a smile. "So, who owns this place? A consortium of gender-bending pianists?"

"What?"

"Your tourist ranch. The Liberace."

Tony looked puzzled. "The Liebe Ranch E. Liebe, love. The Love Ranch. Location 'E' in the franchise."

Jordan laughed. "What's the brand? A candelabra?"

Tony frowned and considered leaving.

"Sorry, Tony. I'm just trying to be funny. But the owners might want to consider skipping the 'E' and going straight to 'F'."

Tony smiled dubiously. "You're the first person that's mentioned it. The German tourists think it's great."

"That makes sense. Didn't Beethoven play piano?"

Then Tony did leave. "Enjoy the party," he said over his shoulder.

A couple that overheard his conversation with Tony were chuckling. He suspected these were friends of Catherine's who might be unsympathetic to her boyfriend. Jord didn't have much action after that.

The third beer was nearing bottom. Catherine had hovered in the kitchen so Jordan hadn't seen her yet. He was planning his escape route to the front door when she popped into the living room and scanned the party. Several people waved at her and she nodded back, smiling. She locked eyes with Jordan and started toward him. The crowd parted to let her pass.

Oh-oh, Jord thought. Here comes that ass-kicking I was promised.

"Tony doesn't like you," she laughed and put her hand on his forearm.

An electric tingle shot up to his shoulder. "I'm sorry. I think our senses of humor are not compatible."

"Tony doesn't have a sense of humor. So no surprise.

Removing her hand, she continued, "How is Heidi doing in class?"

"Caught up. She's bright, just needed practice."

"Yeah. Her rowing is about back to where it was. She's healing." Catherine looked around. "Gotta circulate. Thanks for coming. Thanks for helping Heidi. And thanks," she chuckled, "for giving Tony a hard time. He takes himself way too seriously."

Jord smiled. "Glad to do all those. But I have to cut out. Thanks for the invite."

She smiled and turned away to greet others.

The lab put together a small test section of laminate, embedded with curved strands of fiber bonded to a small sheet of airframe-rated aluminum alloy, and sandwiching their modified hex core. The fiber-bonded aluminum was the process that Jordan hoped to incorporate within his thesis. He had developed his algorithm in small spurts of effort, and was ready to compare it to a real test of real mixed materials.

A small factory, forty miles from the university, manufactured pontoons to adapt light airplanes for amphibious use. Lab students discovered this facility and had enlisted the factory's willing assistance in vacuum bagging and baking composite test samples. When it came later to constructing the actual boat, the lab would have to build their own bagging system and oven, because the rowing shell was longer than the pontoons and would not fit the factory equipment. Some of the students were already at work, building a furnace with thin, recycled sheet steel, refractory wool, and six heating elements salvaged from discarded domestic kitchen ovens. They also used the thermostats and switches.

"So," Jordan asked Heidi at the end of Monday's tutoring session, "you're going home this Wednesday for Thanksgiving?"

"No. I don't think I'm ready to face my family yet without breaking down. Even if I didn't, they'd know something was off and hound me to death. I told them a good friend had invited me, and I'd be with her."

"But you won't?"

Heidi shook her head. "I'm planning a retreat. I've had enough pressure for a while. The apartment will be empty, and I'll be able to let the world go to hell without me for a few days. How about you?"

"Same here. My family is in Flagstaff, and it's too far to drive, even if I had a car. The plane ticket is too much money. And I sure won't miss the family arguments."

Heidi said, "I guess Coach is going to see Tony. Get in some skiing."

Jordan grimaced. "So I hear."

Heidi smiled, but with sympathy.

They sat quietly a moment until Heidi began gathering her stuff into the backpack.

"Say," Jordan said as revelation took him. "How about, for Thanksgiving dinner, I whip up an old recipe I got from a college roommate, and we can eat together? Simple thing. Two turkey legs with the shanks cut off, popped into the slow-cooker with vegetables and spices. Throw together a salad. A small loaf of home baked bread. It's great and takes no effort. Around three in the afternoon?"

Heidi could see disruption threatening her retreat. "I really was looking for the time off."

"Just the meal. Sit down at three, eat, chat, try to figure out if we have something worth being thankful for, and call it a day."

She frowned, hesitated, but said, "Okay. A meal." She stood, swung the pack to her shoulder and went.

Heidi arrived at a quarter to three. Jordan, true to his promise, sat her at the table and dished food. He offered a glass of fruity wine with the food, disclaiming any desire to corrupt her with illegal drink at her tender age of nineteen.

She said, "I'll be twenty on December twenty-first."

"But you won't be twenty-one."

"I have wine with the family at special meals. This qualifies."

So she had a glass with him and they thought about potentially thank-worthy aspects of their lives. They joked about their gratitude for antibiotics and modern dentistry, but became serious when they considered what the world would be like without these. No surprise, they both put Catherine at the top of their thanksgiving lists.

Heidi left at five thirty, thanking Jordan for the meal and the restful interlude.

Full and alone in the comforting smells of the foods that had simmered all day in the slow-cooker, Jordan sipped his refilled glass of wine and started The Magnificent Seven, swearing that he would watch the whole thing this time.

He called her on Saturday. "You okay?"

"Yup."

"Good. See you Monday."

"Yup."

The boat project was beyond design and into realization, so Jordan had no cause to contact Catherine. Heidi was doing surprisingly well, so that could not be an excuse. And, though he suffered from the lack of contact with the lovely redhead, he was glad for the directed effort he could put into his master's program. He was frustrated by the inability of his algorithm to accurately predict failure in the samples that the lab had tested to destruction.

On December seventh, eight in the evening, he labored at the computer comparing results with predictions, checking his math, and staring at lines of code until his brain threatened to squirt out of his ears.

He heard a light step in the hall, a rap at his office door, and Catherine said, "You need to learn to dance and I need a partner. Let's go."

In the Topping Bar she led him onto the floor away from their table of abandoned, beckoning drinks. "It's called swing, it's fun, and it's great exercise."

Jord groaned.

"And it won't kill you to learn. Hold your left hand out like this. I lay my right into it. Don't clutch, just cup it. Now put your right against my back. Lower. Okay, I put my left hand on your shoulder, and rest my left elbow outside the crook of your right. This gives us good contact to communicate our moves. Watch my feet and mirror what I do."

After a time, when it seemed he had the basic steps, she said, "Let's speed it up to match the music."

Eventually she instructed, "You're the lead, so apply pressure with your left palm to let me know where you want to go, and start us moving around the floor."

This isn't that bad, Jord thought, and then said to Catherine, "This isn't that bad."

"Told you. Now we'll learn another step. Watch."

He was still clumsy when they broke for a rest and drinks, but surprised that it was easier than it looked.

"Pretty good for the first time," Catherine said.

They breathed and cooled down.

Jord asked, "How was your Thanksgiving?"

"Great. Lot's of skiing and other sports. I hear you had a quiet meal."

"Heidi is good company."

"Are you falling for her?"

He glanced at Catherine, then away, and shook his head. "No. I like her, but I've already fallen hard for another woman." And he looked directly into Catherine's eyes without blinking.

She studied his face. "That's what I thought. But I wanted to make sure. Let's dance."

On the way to his apartment, in her car, she said, "That was fun. It's nice that you're as tall as I am. Tony is a tad short for graceful teamwork. And he moves okay, but he can't feel the rhythm of the music like you do. This could be the beginning of a beautiful friendship."

"No," Jordan said. "None of that crap. If you're going to quote 'Casablanca' say, 'play it, Sam'. Friendship is not all I'm looking for."

"I know," she laughed. "And I'm thinking that's okay."

She dropped him in the parking lot of the apartments and drove off as he levitated to his rooms. He, too, was thinking that's okay.

Two days later she phoned. "Should I pick you up at seven?"

"Sure," Jord said. "For what?"

"The three D's—dining, drinking and dancing."

"What about the fourth D? Dutch?"

"You can pay if you want, but don't think it buys privileges."

"Actually," Jord said, "you're the one making a good salary. Why don't you pay? And ignore privileges."

"Cheapskate. Hell, let's go dutch and sort out the privileges later."

"Suits me."

When they sorted out the privileges later at his apartment, he discovered that she liked to go slow, to linger, to luxuriate. It was the best sex he had ever had.

They spent five more evenings sharing privileges and becoming delightfully familiar.

The next week in the Topping Bar they sat against each other at a small table, letting their breathing moderate after that last dance, getting liquids to replace perspiration, when she said, "You know, if we got blood tests, we could stop using condoms."

"What?!" He spewed beer and coughed.

"Listen," she scowled, "I'm not saying I want to marry you. It's just that if we both knew it was safe, we could ditch the condoms, enjoy it more, be more spontaneous. I use other birth control. Granted, it means exclusivity, and we *both* have to be deadly serious about that."

"What about Christmas break?"

By which she understood he was asking, 'What about Tony'.

She said, "Two things. One, I decided to spend Christmas break here. And, two, Tony has never had freedom from condoms, and never will."

"Then why me?"

"Tony is an opportunist. I think you're more steady. Am I right?"

"When do we go to the clinic?"

Catherine and the sculling team put together a birthday party for Heidi's twentieth, celebrated early to get it in before the term broke for Christmas. The three rowing teams were there and the junior ME lab was invited to make it a nice, casual mixer. The lab students, particularly the men, were intimidated by the long, strong women scullers, but everybody felt the exciting potential of the new boat and, with this in common, they mingled comfortably. One particularly cute coxswain became the focus of several of the lab men.

After the party broke-up and everybody had gone, Jordan and Catherine relaxed on her couch with wine glasses, her head of impossibly colored hair leaning on his shoulder.

Jordan said, "Heidi's going home for the break."

"She feels ready, and they could get suspicious if she didn't go this time."

They sipped in silence.

Catherine said, "You know you're the only man she told?"

"No. I didn't."

"When you first started this boat thing, I thought you were just another asshole wanting to get into my pants and using the boat and Heidi to do it."

"I was," he chuckled. "And, hey, it worked!"

"Yeah, like I said, asshole. But you treated Heidi right when she needed it. I began to think there might be more to you."

"Well." But he was too embarrassed to say more.

They relished the quiet and the shared pressure of their bodies.

Jord said, "It's just a shame the monster that hurt Heidi got off Scot-free."

Catherine sipped her wine and made a little smile that he couldn't see.

Free Body Diagram

That Christmas break surpassed any other period in Jordan's life. He had given up believing perfection could be possible. His disastrous marriage to The Evil One had been his yardstick of relationships, and it was a poor measure.

He spent his days contentedly working on the intractable problem of his algorithm, and his evenings with the amazing Catherine. When the band was in at the Topping Bar, they danced. The rest of the evenings they spent at his apartment, either dining in or returning there after dining out, a bottle of wine with a classic movie, including Casablanca twice, and usually ending with protracted love-making.

She liked having her own space so she showered and drove home around midnight. This is why they preferred his place for each other's company, so she, the one with the car, could reclaim her solitude. She once asked if he wanted to join her in the shower and he said, "No, I like waking up with your scent all over me." Despite the translucence of her complexion it was the only time he had ever seen her blush.

Christmas eve she slept over and in the morning they exchanged gifts. He gave her a Bill Bryson book about Australia, and she gave him a small Swiss-army knife that included scissors, nail file, tooth pick and, ta-da!, a cork-screw. He sensed her self-interest in that last.

New Years Eve they danced at their usual haunt, drank to the shared joy, drank to themselves and sang Auld Lang Syne (at least the first five words because it's all either knew) toasting the new year.

They had left Catherine's car at his apartment and walked to the bar. She rarely had more than a couple of drinks, but they wanted to make sure they would not have to curtail it if she felt like more. She felt like. After they had rung in the new year they yearned to celebrate alone, so they walked to Jord's.

She flopped on the couch and said, "I think I left something in your fridge yesterday. Could you get it for me?"

"Sure." He didn't know when she could have sneaked them in, but he found there a bottle of good, dry champagne and two fine glasses. He sat across the coffee table from her and poured.

They already felt silly drunk and soon lapsed into giddy.

"Okay," Catherine said. "It's that time in our relationship to deepen the trust we started with the condom thing. And we're primed." She lifted her freshly filled glass.

"Fine. How do we do that?"

"We tell each other a true story about ourselves that we have never told another soul."

Jordan, a fiercely private person, prone to easy embarrassment, did not like this idea, even drunk. She could tell he was reluctant.

"Come on, Jord. It's now or never, and you get to start."

"Does it have to be really horrible, or just untellable in usual company?"

"That second thing as long as it's the first telling. We can get more devilish another time. Fess up. And remember, we are vowing to never repeat what we hear."

He thought a while, staring at his bubbling drink, and remembered the story.

"College, my sophomore year. I roomed in a tiny apartment with a friend I had known since fifth grade. We, along with many other hopeful young men, haunted the bars in foolish belief that this is how you met women. Eventually the regular crowd of strangers becomes a crowd of acquaintances, but you rarely or never meet women interested in meeting you.

Among those we got to know pretty well was a portion of the lesbian crowd that hung out together. Sometimes my old chum and I would pull our table over and join the lesbians in raucous drinking. Everybody got along nicely. One of the young ladies appealed greatly to me and I developed a crush. Yes," Jordan said at Catherine's look, "tilting at windmills. But it was obvious that she liked me, too, in a different light. It took me two months to realize that one of the reasons they let us into their company was because they thought my roommate and I were a gay couple. I'm slow on the uptake. You see, we always cruised the bar together, and had known each other for so long that we finished each other's sentences..."

"And," Catherine interrupted, "you are strangely sensitive, for a straight man."

"Don't get me started on *that* curse. Well, during one bout of drunkenness at the communal table, we discovered that the lesbian contingent had never seen Night of the Living Dead. They knew Dawn of the Living Dead, but not the black-and-white cult-classic that had originally set the tone. We offered to give them a viewing at our place, since the video held a position of honor in our collection. Three of them agreed, including the target of my misled crush."

Catherine shook her head as she sensed where this was leading.

"I served beers all around and started the video. In ten minutes my prospective love, sitting on pillows on the floor at the end of the ratty love-seat, passed out and crumpled into the corner of the room. My buddy and I remained transfixed by the movie. The other two women had enough after the first beer and left, not noticing their third member passed out in the corner.

"The movie ended. I discovered my erstwhile darling. She looked comfortable enough wedged in the pillows, and I couldn't think of an option better than letting her sleep it off right there. It was a *really* tiny apartment. My bed was in the video room, in fact it's where my roomy and I had sat to watch the movie. He trundled off to the only real bedroom. I visited the bathroom, returned and flopped on my bed."

Catherine began to cringe.

"Should I stop?"

"No. I have to hear the rest."

"Some time in the night my beauty awoke, sleepwalked into the bathroom for a pee and returned to the only bed available. I sensed a body joining me and jolted awake. Then froze. She lay on her side, faced away from me, fully clothed, including shoes, and spooned into me, instantly asleep. I too, because of her presence in my room, had remained clothed, though shoe-less. Well, and this is the most embarrassing part, that warm female body felt pretty damned good tucked into me, so I just let her stay."

"Oh, no," Catherine whispered.

"In hindsight, I know I should have crawled over her and bunked on the love seat, but didn't. It took me quite a while to fall back to sleep in this novel situation. When I woke again it was because a very surprised lesbian had discovered my arm draped over her waist and my friendly hand clasped against her belly, innocently north of her navel and south of her breasts."

Catherine put a hand to her mouth, either in horror or to restrain a laugh.

"Remember, she still had her shoes on. She stomped the hell out of me and only slowed down when she noticed those shoes, and her clothes, and my clothes. 'Fucker!' she spat at me and disappeared. I never saw her again. I heard she left town, but assume it was unrelated."

"That's perfect!" Catherine chortled.

Jordan poured them each another glass of sparkling wine. "Your turn," he said.

"Remember.   Not a word to anybody, under any circumstance."

"I swear."

"Okay."   She dropped her eyes to her glass, but lifted them again, wanting to witness Jord's reaction.   "My story is shorter, but more horrible. I gathered a cohort of strong women and beat the shit out of a rapist. And left him with a broom handle in his ass to make sure he understood and would remember."

Jordan waited a moment with a silly grin on his face for the punch line to this story. Then he frowned. "That's it?"

"What more do you need? Details?"

"No, but...You really did that?"

"Yes. Now, if we were eight year old boys, we'd have to cut our palms, clasp hands and swear mutual fealty as blood-brothers. Or blood-lovers in our case."

"Wow."

They had been seated across from each other.   Jordan stood and stepped around the coffee table to sit beside her on the couch. "Wow," he said again, leaning to put his arm around her shoulders. "Good for you."

Neither of them expected her to drive home after the volume of drink they had overcome together, so they slept entwined in his bed. She began snoring immediately while he lay awake, head spinning with the champagne and the incredible story she had told. It occurred to him that the rapist who had absorbed justice from her hands was surely the monster that had hurt Heidi. A warm pride infused him. She was some woman. Probably Heidi's crew had helped, though he wondered about Heidi. That could have backfired and caused her more trauma. He would ask Catherine.

Very late the next morning, after he had sectioned some grapefruit, basted some eggs and burnt some toast for their breakfast, and they had eaten, while Catherine cocooned on the couch with a coffee and Smithsonian magazine, Jordan went on-line to pull up the archives of the local newspaper. He searched around the time of Heidi's disappearance from class. There it was, the only story that fit. "Fallen Star Tackle Won't Finish Season. Gerard 'Grid' Deimos, 21, tackle for State University, took a hard fall on his fraternity steps Saturday. He suffered several broken bones and will not finish the season." The article went on to include his sporting accomplishments, speculation about his great future in football, but no mention of an attack by angry women or a broom handle up the ass.

Given the date of Grid's "fall", Heidi could not have been involved. She could not have recovered from needing help dressing herself to assaulting her attacker in only six days. Catherine had mentioned that they could "handle" it over the weekend. He printed the article.

The returned school schedule did not dampen Jord and Catherine's relationship, but it did reduce opportunities to indulge it. They cut back to dancing only Thursdays and Saturdays and spent the evening together on Monday because neither had early morning commitments on Tuesday. The intensity of Jordan's emotions only increased, and he believed, hoped, that Catherine's were rising to match. He was not wrong.

Catherine, burdened with beauty, had encountered many men, all of them carrying just one thing in mind, or somewhere. The difference with Jordan was that it was not the *only* thing in his mind. Or his heart. His combination of intelligence and kindness overcame any lack he suffered in assertiveness. Though, too, she remembered calling him a pushy bastard. Okay, she also knew that she was letting herself in for emotional involvement when she made the "sans condom" offer. Requirements for a degree in physical education had evolved over the decades from a basic ability to learn exercise routines, the body parts they strengthened, and how to force students into them. Her training was so complete that she could have easily stepped into the path toward a medical degree. So she knew that semen carried hormones which fired a woman's sense of love for her partner. She suspected that Jordan Winslow was worth the risk.

Heidi returned refreshed from her visit home. She had not broken down, nor suffered suspicious scrutiny, and seemed almost like her old confident self.

When Catherine and Jordan discussed Heidi's return to normalcy, she explained that the most lasting damage was that lack of confidence. "The bruises heal. The violation can diminish with time, but you never get over the sense that you have no control in your life, your own destiny. Kids are encouraged, protected and cherished, and spoiled. They think the world is a kind place, that they make the decisions, and that they can be whatever they want to be. Then a rapist takes all of that away, and it never comes back."

"Never?" Jord asked.

"Studies show that the most dangerous health stressor is lack of control in your own life. It's a major feature of mammalian character. You can't escape it."

The mold for the hull was done. With six parallel heating circuits the oven held to two degrees variation, not professional quality but adequate.

Tests indicated that the oars might or might not benefit from the whale lumps, but that the stabilizing fin definitely would. They eliminated the rudder by also delegating steering to the fin. This cleaned up the fluid flow remarkably. It was their largest gain for a single design change.

They began laying up the laminate.

Heidi, having completed dynamics with a respectable three point eight, was not in Jordan's class this semester. She showed up in his office at the end of the third week. "So, how are you at calculus?" she asked him.

"I love calculus. In my mediocre college career, I excelled at calculus."

"Would you be cool with tutoring me?"

"Just ask."

"I just did. I'll post you my schedule."

He gave her a smile and a snappy military salute.

Though she didn't mention it to Jordan, Catherine received several recriminating phone calls from Tony because of her no-show at Vail for Christmas. She kept it civil, but reminded him of the "non-possessive" nature of their relationship and told him that she didn't feel like maintaining even that little bit of claim.

"Is it the boat-guy?" Tony asked.

"Yes."

"He's a geek."

"Yes," she agreed, "a bright, sensitive, caring geek. Lacking all of the qualities needed to fuck a hutch-full of ski-bunnies."

"This makes him better?"

"That depends on your, or in this case, my definition of better. Since I'm the one in a position to judge, yes. It makes him better."

The broken connection signaled Tony's goodbye for that conversation, but they had several more. It seemed Tony was suffering that old "good for the goose, good for the gander" dilemma.

The shell popped cleanly out of the mold. The other parts were carefully joined to the hull. Setbacks delayed the work, but there are always setbacks and they were overcome. Errors delayed the work because everybody involved was human, but those were corrected. Dedicated students buffed the finished boat to a mirror luster. The date set for the first rowing test was February twelfth, weather permitting.

"I'm sorry," Catherine told Jordan, "but he didn't give me any warning. He just showed up."

The season at Vail was slowing. Tony decided to take a break in the slack period but return before the Presidents Day weekend when business surged. A friend covered his ski lessons for him and he drove straight through to Evansville without sleeping.

"He knew we were launching the boat," Jordan stated.

"It came up..."

"During one of your regular phone calls. Did anything else 'come up'? Like us?"

She scowled. "We are on the verge of our first fight."

"Then we'd better get it over with so we can move on to our second fight."

If he had used just a slightly different tone or facial expression she would have lit into him properly. Instead she laughed. "Okay. I've been talking to him, but I'm not the one who calls. And I have made it as clear as possible that his part in my life is over. But he's having more trouble letting go than I expected."

"And why does he have to hang around your place?"

"I can't just send him to a motel. For God's sake, we had a long relationship. The least I can do is let him sleep in the guest room." Jordan lifted an eyebrow. Catherine's anger rose at that and she said flatly, "Remember mutual trust? Are you tossing it out so soon?"

He smiled. "No," he said. "I believe you. Jealousy is not a voluntary response. I trust you. Please accept the jealousy as a proof of my love."

"You are a goofy sentimentalist."

"Why don't you just lend him the house and stay at my place?"

"Let him drive me out of my own home?"

"What was I thinking?" Jord asked.

Free Body Diagram

It is not easy to maintain athletic discipline during a momentous launching. Somebody even suggested breaking a bottle of champagne on, or near the bow of the new craft. This was quashed as too grand, risky for the boat, dangerous to future barefoot strollers, and an unnecessary delay. The first crew, Heidi's crew, cheerfully humped the shell to the dock, hefted it overhead and splooched it onto the water. A small but exuberant cheer punctuated the boat's virginal touch to the river. The weather cooperated with one of those sunny February days that gives people hope that they will survive to spring.

The boat was already loaded with strain gauges and the tiny device that simultaneously recorded the data and transmitted it to the laptop in the pilot boat. The same six cameras were rigged that had studied the old shell. Professor Durning had become interested during the project, so even he had shown for the test, and was double-checking proper placement of the test equipment.

The lab students verified the data collection system operation while the women made a warm-up run to the far end of the course. Everything was working nicely and no part of the boat registered anywhere near failure so they turned and aimed back at the dock from two thousand meters. This was going to be a timed, full-out, competition level run.

Catherine had placed spotters along the course to signal her when the boat passed, and each time a flag dropped she glanced at her stopwatch, and each time she glanced at her stopwatch she grew more excited. At a thousand meters she couldn't hold "The Bellow" in any longer. "Pull!" she volleyed. "Pull your guts out! Can you hear me?!"

Grid's sphincter puckered and he froze. He knew that voice. The football hit him in the ribs and he didn't feel it.

Last October Grid had found himself surrounded in the dark while crossing the track field. He had suffered injuries and indignities that he would never, as long as he lived, divulge to anybody. With his good arm he had reached behind, still sobbing after the zip-ties were gone, and removed the broomstick. It hurt more coming out than going in. That suggested a degree of damage that he couldn't contemplate yet in his state of shock. He had struggled up, hurting his broken arm badly, and, when balanced precariously, tugged his pants up with the good arm, this time creating agony in the fractured collarbone. Unable to fasten them with one hand, he held them together and staggered toward the frat house. The broomstick, streaked for six inches along one side with a narrow line of blood, lay abandoned to confuse a jogger the next day.

He defied the insistence of his fraternity brothers until he'd had a chance, in private, to make certain that he was not completely ripped open. The bleeding was already reduced and he was able to staunch it and clean himself a bit. He pulled on clean underwear and pants, finally succumbing to the need for help in buttoning and zipping the pants, and in getting a ride to the emergency room.

The emergency room doctor was obviously not buying it, but Grid stuck to the story about falling down the steps. They set his arm, put a sling on the other to hold his clavicle together, and they ignored his cracked cheekbone. They shot him full of antibiotics for his bitten tongue and gave him a prescription for more. He felt relieved that he would not have to make some excuse to get a shot to ward off infection from his real injury.

The police had stopped by the frat house the next day, but he stuck to the story. Eventually his disgrace ceased to be the most interesting house topic, and it faded. His inner shame and his fury did not.

The cast had come off his arm in December. By mid January he could toss the football around with his house brothers. They took advantage of the sunny February twelfth to go down to Riverbend park and run some patterns.

Then he heard the voice.

Grid looked down at the river and walked off toward a group there. One of his friends called, "Hey, Grid. Where you going?"

He ignored them.

"At least throw the ball back!"

Grid gave them the finger without even looking behind. He got close enough to distinguish features in the small crowd at the dock, but he held back near a tree to avoid notice. Not likely that they would look around; everybody was fixed with excitement on the slim boat racing toward them. It didn't take long to identify the source of "the voice" as the woman with brilliant red hair. He studied her until the boat crossed the finish and turned to approach the jubilant people on shore. As it drew close and slid beside the dock he also recognized the girl, rowing in the bow, as the stubborn date he'd had the week before his humiliation. Now it was clear.

He had met the girl studying at the student union building Saturday afternoon and chatted her up, then invited her for a burger and a movie. She had led him on all evening with her smiles and her little "shy", sideways glances, but as they neared her apartment and his hands began to test the waters she started pushing his hands and him away. The rage that always lurked just below his surface erupted and he wrestled her aside into a small stand of trees. She was tough and strong so it took quite a few solid thumps to get her to relax and give up what she'd been promising all night. Then, after he had left her there, she'd obviously gone home and whined to the big redhead. Yes, it was all clear.

The crews, the coach and the lab students were literally jumping for joy. Catherine had bellowed over the water to the boat as it crossed the line, "A record! Six seconds faster than your best! Yeee-haw!"

The boat reached the dock, the rowers boiled out of it, nearly capsizing, and joined the hugging, backslapping bunch.

"And this is the guy responsible," Catherine yelled. "Jordan!"

One of the crew began a chant, "Jor-DAN, Jor-DAN." They all took it up and pressed around him. They lifted him onto their shoulders and bounced him in rhythm to the chant. With one mind, they shuffled toward the river, ignoring his yells of, "NO! NO!", and pitched him into the thirty-three degree water. He surfaced, gasping from the cold and sucked in a splash of water so that he was choking and sputtering as he swam four strokes to the dock and was hoisted out by laughing admirers.

"Holy shit!" he shrieked. "God damn that's cold!"

They had towels, blankets and heat-packs on hand for just such an accidental immersion, so they tossed a blanket around his shoulders and told him to strip to his underwear, which he reluctantly did. Somebody at the front yelled back to the others, "Tighty-whities!" And they all laughed. They wrapped him in towels and stuffed activated heat-packs into them, then re-wrapped him in a new, dry blanket.

Jordan was not pleased with this unanticipated result to the success of his boat. If he could have foreseen it, he would have been well away from the celebrants when the boat returned. It did cheer him back up, though, to have his lovely Catherine hug him tightly and kiss him hard.

Tony, unhappily hovering through it all at the perimeter, looked even less happy at this display. He turned away from everyone and walked to the parking lot.

Grid Deimos strode back up the hill to rejoin his frat brothers.

The crew tossed together an impromptu party at Catherine's, and she and Jordan, the old, responsible adults, turned a blind eye to the champagne consumed by crew and lab members who still fell short of twenty-one years age.

Catherine raised her glass and shouted, "A toast to Jord. And his tighty-whities."

Everybody laughed. "JORD!"

He put on a brave smile illumined with a blush.

"To six seconds," one of the rowers toasted.

"SIX SECONDS."

Then Jord raised his glass toward Heidi's crew and said, "To Catherine and her four oarsmen of the apocalypse."

The lab students laughed. Heidi's crew smiled mildly and the rest of the crew rolled their eyes, but everybody drank.

"That's not original, Jord," Catherine said in his ear.

"It is to me. I just thought of it."

"But we," she gestured at her crews, " have been rowing for years. Don't think you're the only punster to pitch it. And don't say anything about scullery maids."

He shrugged and clinked his glass to hers. "To us then," he whispered.

"To us, and to the removal of your tighty-whities."

Tony dutifully raised his glass to each toast, but he still hadn't cheered up. Though the party shut down early to get the illegally young drinkers out and home, he had already retreated to the guest room and consoled himself with a call to one of his former ski students whom he knew would be coming up to Vail for a refresher course over Presidents Day weekend.

Catherine drove Jord home and was in too good a mood to go back to her house after their warm, celebratory love-making, especially knowing that Tony was still there.

Sunday, mid-morning they kissed goodbye and she said, as she was leaving, "I think Tony will understand it's over with him. I'll stress the point before he goes. See you Monday after work."

Jordan dawdled the rest of the afternoon at correcting the papers he had ignored so he could participate in the boat test. Noting the dates on the papers he realized that Monday would be Valentine's Day. He would have to arrange something special for their evening together.

He called Catherine about nine thirty that night but she didn't answer. She was probably in the shower, so he sent her a goodnight text, read for forty-five minutes, killed the light and lay down to a peaceful sleep.

Free Body Diagram

The classroom echoed quiet. The classroom echoed emptiness. Jordan walked through the door and dropped his textbook and notes on the lectern, plugged the projector into his laptop and booted it up. He was cleaning the white-board and heard the squeak of athletic shoe on polished floor. He turned to greet whichever student had nothing better to do than show up five minutes early for his class. Heidi stood there with a face of such distress, horror and grief that Jordan's own face went pale.

"Heidi," he said, going to her, "what's wrong?"

"She's dead!"

"Who? Who's dead?" he asked, but regretted the question. He didn't want to know. If he didn't know, it didn't happen. It couldn't have happened.

She fell against him, pressed her face to his shoulder. "Coach," she whispered and shuddered with a gasping cry. "Coach is dead!"

His brain began to shut down. "No, Heidi. That can't be."

She just sobbed against him, and the habits remaining as he retreated inside made him wrap his arms around her in comfort. Words could not form. His sense of time vanished and he was explosive when the first student stepped into the classroom. Jordan pierced him with such a look of furious anguish that the mocking smile, at catching the TA in a "situation", disappeared and he jerked to a stop. Jordan gestured and the student backed out.

"Shut it!"

The door closed.

"Heidi, we have to go. Here, sit while I get my stuff." Habit had to take over. Shock had driven his mind into a dark corner and all that remained was a simple routine of If-Then statements. If Catherine is dead, then I must go. If I must go, then I must collect my things.

He packed his computer, notes, and textbook into his New Yorker tote bag.

"Come on," he said, taking Heidi's hand to lift her out of the desk. "We have to leave."

Outside the door he looked in confusion at the group standing in the hall, warned off by the first student with, "Winslow looks like he's going to rip somebody's throat out. I wouldn't go in there."

If he must go, then class is over. "Class is canceled," Jordan said to the air. "Go away."

Jordan couldn't walk. He stood frozen in front of the building with a bag in his left hand and his right reflexively holding Heidi to him. The first step of that mile to his apartment overwhelmed him. Stricken, he looked around, waiting for the world to stop, to go away, but it didn't. In what was either an eternity or a second, he set down his bag and pulled his phone from a pocket. He thumbed until he found local services and punched "taxi".

"In front of the," he looked behind them, "general engineering building on campus."

It barely registered that the car stopping at the curb was supposed to take them home. Winslow helped Heidi into the taxi and slid in beside her. If I am in a taxi, then I must give an address. He automatically gave the location of his apartment.

He never recovered the bag abandoned on the sidewalk.

Free Body Diagram

The cab had driven a couple of blocks when Jordan surfaced long enough to ask Heidi, "How did it happen?"

"Killed." She put her face in her hands. "Beat to death."

"But... That's crazy. How, why?"

She looked up. "I don't know. That's all Beth told us."

"There has to be more than that. Driver! Take us by the Whole Health Building, please. You think she's still there, Heidi?"

"Probably. She looked ready to faint, and I bet she wants to find a dark hole for a while, but there'll be a lot of calls coming in and she has to handle them."

They rode silently until the cab stopped. They paid, got out and Jordan asked the cabbie, "Can you wait?"

"This is a tow-away zone."

"Okay. Here's five bucks. Cruise around the block slow and we'll catch you when we're done. It won't be long."

The driver shrugged, tucked the bill in his shirt pocket and said, "Okay. But five bucks don't buy much cruising."

They stopped outside the office door and saw Beth, the assistant coach, at her desk with her head lying on her arms. They knocked lightly. Beth raised her head. She wasn't crying now, but she had been.

"Jordan, Heidi," she said. "It's horrible."

"You okay?" Jordan asked.

"No, I'm not. I'll never be okay again." She shuddered and, if possible, became even more pale.

"What happened?"

"I don't know. Somebody snuck in Catherine's back door and... God it was horrible."

"You found her?"

"Yes." She closed her eyes. "I can't stop seeing it. Blood everywhere. Her face, her head.... Oh, God!"

"Are you sure it was her? Did you check?"

"I didn't even go in the house. Didn't have to. Nobody else has hair like Catherine's. It was her. But that was the only way to tell. Nothing else was left."

"What do you mean, 'nothing else was left'?"

"Just that. Her face was destroyed."

"Who, for Chris'sake, could do this? And why?"

Beth shook her head. "We worked together three years. She was a sister. I wish I could stop seeing her like that."

"Where did they take her?"

Beth shrugged. "Hospital morgue, I guess. Nothing to be done for her." Then she started crying again. Heidi numbly knelt by the chair and hugged her.

Jordan said, "I'm going to see what the police say. Are you staying with Beth, Heidi?"

"Are you okay on your own, Beth?" Heidi asked.

"Alone or not. Doesn't matter. Go. See if you can find out what the hell happened."

Heidi stood, rested her hand briefly on Beth's shoulder, then left with Jordan.

The cab was making its third swing around the big block when they left the building. It pulled to the curb and let them in. "Where to?" The driver asked.

"Police station."

The police receptionist asked, "How can I help you?"

"What do you know about the murder of Catherine Sinjohn?"

"And who are you?"

"Close friends of Catherine's."

"I'm sorry. We haven't been able to reach the victim's family, yet. Until then, we can't release any information."

"Was it really her?" Heidi asked.

"Sorry, miss. We can't even confirm or deny identity until next-of-kin is notified."

"But you know it's her?" Jordon asked.

"A positive I.D. has been made with fingerprints and dental records. If you contact us in a day or two, we can provide more information."

They could think of no better persuasion, so they returned to the taxi.

"One more stop," Jordon told the driver. "Memorial Hospital."

They fared no better at the hospital. No, they couldn't see the body, and would regret it if they did. No information could be released pending notification of next-of-kin. Jordan tried claiming that he was Catherine's brother, but the clerk asked for I.D. and they left in frustration.

The patient taxi stood waiting. "Home then," Jordan said, and gave his address to the cabbie.

They stepped out at his apartment building, he paid the driver, unaware that he had tipped too much, and it was only when he unlocked his front door and opened it for Heidi that he realized she was still with him and that he had not sent her home. He grew more exhausted and helpless with every step. They sat on his old couch, separate for a time and then Heidi turned to him and he circled his arms protectively again, wishing someone could do the same for him.

It was very dark. Jordan noticed the glow of the streetlight and understood that it had grown late.

"Heidi," he said, "we need to get you home."

"I can't move."

He looked at her face, lit by the dim orange light, striated in crystal trails of desiccated tears. She had stopped crying. He noticed the crusted feel of his own cheeks.

"At least we need food. Something to drink."

He felt her shrug.

Jordan gently pushed her away to sit upright. He stumped into the kitchen and saw the box of crackers. Why not? He couldn't fix real food. The cheese sat in its usual place in the fridge. He gathered two bottles of water, the cheese knife and a plate to hold it all. These went to the coffee table and he returned to the kitchen to pick a couple of oranges from a bag on the counter. Jord and Heidi sat opposite over the coffee table. He gave her the knife and she began. The knife passed back and forth alternately.

After a time, Jordan put the knife down, hung his head forward and tears leaked out. They dripped off his nose to the table, making dark, growing stars that merged into a spreading, irregular stain—a Rorschach test of his grief.

Heidi watched him while pools formed at the corners of her own eyes. He stopped crying and wiped his face for the umpteenth time. Heidi picked up a cracker, sliced a token sliver of cheese, placed it on the cracker, and set it upon his knee.

They looked at each other through watery eyes. He ate the cracker.

"Take the bed," Jord said. "The sheets are clean. I was expecting..." He pinched the bridge of his nose. "Anyway, there are toiletries in the bathroom. Shower, whatever. Towels are in that closet. You'll find new toothbrushes and toothpaste in the vanity. Grab a cup from the kitchen."

While the bathroom sounds murmured he sat in the dark staring through the window at the distant streetlight.

The noises behind him stopped. Heidi crossed quietly barefooted to the bedroom and paused at the door. "What about tomorrow?'

"What tomorrow."

All night Heidi lay awake worrying about the dire implications of 'what tomorrow'. She got up once to see him sitting on the couch with the afghan around his shoulders, staring out the window. It felt strange to her, for a change, to be the one ready to offer comfort.

Daylight overpowered the streetlight. This clue jogged Jordan into the one action that he knew must come next, by virtue of "if-then". His sleepless night had not given him more than that. The clock said seven-twenty. James deWitt picked up on the second ring. "James," Jordan said, "can you and Dave take my classes for the next week? Maybe two?"

"Jord. Sure. I don't... God, I heard about it at school. Jesus Christ. Take the time you need. You're covered."

"Thanks."

It was light enough in the kitchen, without switching on lights, that he could prime the coffee maker. The steam eruptions began driving hot water into the filter cone as he closed the bathroom door to get his own shower. It would not replace the sleep, or ease the ache behind his eyes, or stop the ringing in his ears or do much else, but it was another step to the ordinary.

Jord was building his signature breakfast of sectioned citrus, burnt toast and basted eggs. Dammit! He had stared too long out the window and the eggs were hard. He hated them hard. "Shit, I hate them hard," he muttered.

He jumped when Heidi, at his shoulder, said, "Looks okay to me." She worked her way around the cupboards, opening one after another. "No," she said, holding up a hand when he spoke to direct her to the plates. "I need a small challenge that I can overcome." She searched through drawers looking for flatware.

Breakfast gave them a chance to begin to try to normalize, or at least figure out how to put on the bold face they would need for the world.

"How did you sleep?" Heidi asked.

"Not at all. How 'bout you?"

"Same."

"Do your ears ring when you don't get enough sleep?"

"No," she said. "But I feel like two porcupines fighting to get out of a burlap bag."

"You need to go home."

"Let me wash the dishes and brush my teeth."

As she scrubbed her molars, Jord called for the taxi. She stepped into the living room, looking around with a sense of unreality. The doorbell rang. It was ten-twelve, Tuesday morning.

"That'll be the cab," Jord said.

They walked together to the door.

The five policemen with drawn guns, when they saw that Jordan Winslow was not holding a weapon, grabbed him, dragged him through the door, forced him to the deck, and piled onto him. They cuffed him and stood while one officer ensured Winslow's docility by pressing an immobilizing foot on the back of his neck. Two policemen grabbed Heidi's arms, turned her around and forced her against the wall beside the doorway. A hand against the back of her head forced her left cheek against the splintery siding. They were bringing her hands together behind her back while an officer studied a picture in his hand.

"That's the missing girl," he said.

They gently turned her around.

"Are you Heidi van Vleet?" the cop with the picture asked.

With this extra shock to her system she just stood, wide eyed.

The cop shouted, "Are you Heidi van Vleet?"

She nodded.

"Has he hurt you?"

She looked confused.

"Has he hurt you, Miss?"

"Who?" she asked.

"Winslow."

She laughed a hysterical chop. "That's crazy! Of course not."

"Has he threatened you in any way?"

She was beginning to reconnect. "That's stupid! What's going on?"

"Is there anybody else in the apartment?"

"No."

Policemen carefully entered to verify its vacancy.

"Are you sure, miss, that he has not hurt you or threatened you?"

"Of course I'm sure. He's my... He's the nicest man I know."

"What were you going to say? 'He's my...'?"

Her eyes darted away and flashed back with fire in them. "He's my teacher! My tutor! My friend!"

The policeman knew that's not what she had planned to say, but his guess was wrong. He assumed 'lover', but she had almost said 'benefactor'. A subconscious brake had locked the word before it slipped out. It was a word that would lead to other questions. How a benefactor? What comfort? A rape? When? Her respect for authority shrank by the second.

She said, "Let him up!"

The officer spoke aside to a fellow. "I guess she's okay. Maybe he's not the guy."

He asked Heidi, "Where have you been since noon yesterday?"

"Why?"

"Your roommates got worried around ten last night, what with...ah...circumstances, and reported you missing. We thought you were in trouble."

"I was with Jor... Mr. Wins... Jordan. I wanted him to hear about Coach from a friend. They're... very close. Then we came here and cried."

"All night? Together?"

"Not *together* all night."

"And not always crying."

"You some kind of pervert? We did NOT have SEX for Chris'sake!"

"Let him up," the cop said.

As they helped Jordan to his feet the cop continued, "Mr. Winslow, this is a warrant to search your apartment. We need to have your key."

"I can't reach it in these handcuffs."

"Which pocket?"

"Front right. Why are you doing this?"

The policeman paused, judging whether he should bother. He took a breath and said, "The rowing coach is murdered. The murder weapon is found leaning against the door of the boat shed. Another woman disappears, a rower. The last time she's seen is leaving campus with you, the present boyfriend of the murder victim. The ex-boyfriend was staying at the victim's house. That would give you motive. The ex has an alibi. That's enough for a warrant."

Jordan shook his head. "I love her. Catherine is the last person on earth I could ever hurt."

"In our experience people are always killed by the ones who love them. Both of you have to come with us to answer some questions."

After the boat test at the park on Saturday, Grid Deimos had grabbed his friend Shawn. "I need your car keys."

"What for?"

"Business."

"How will me and Benji get back to the house?"

"Jump in the back of Will's truck."

"And freeze our asses off?"

"You'll live. Keys."

Shawn grudgingly handed them over and said, "You owe me one."

"No." Grid said, pocketing the keys. "You owe me one less."

Deimos located Shawn's ratty Honda Civic and settled in to wait.

The sculling crowd wanted to shift their celebration to a more comfortable location, so it wasn't long before they trooped around the corner of the boat shed and spread through the parking lot to find their cars. The big, red-headed woman and the guy, Jordan, that they'd thrown into the river, climbed into a green VW bug. Cars left, strung out as a loose group. Grid followed at a distance watching the VW keep on as some of them peeled off at the supermarket. Eventually the bug took a right turn while the rest continued, so he followed the VW, which made a couple more turns then pulled into apartment parking. He drove beyond a short distance, stopped and watched them walk to a particular door. Grid drove around the block and parked on the street close enough to see both the door and the car. Apparently Jordan and Red lived here. He looked at his phone: Three-thirty. It was early enough to sit and see if they would come out again.

Fifteen minutes later the pair left the building laughing together and climbed into the green Beetle. They came back down the street toward him so he ducked his head a bit as if he was texting.

"That's refreshing," Jordan said.

"What?" Catherine asked.

"That guy back there was texting, but parked instead of driving."

"I guess there are some reasonable people in the world after all."

Grid waited until they were almost out of sight, and made a U-turn. He broke the speed limit to catch back up. They turned east on Orchard. In about three miles Grid glanced down at the dashboard where a new light had caught his attention. That damned Shawn never bought more than a couple gallons of gas at a time. The VW drove until they neared the city limit and then ducked around a few corners, finally pulling up at an older house surrounded by most of the cars that had been at Riverbend Park. Again Grid parked discretely.

It was obviously a party. Grid glanced at his phone again. Still a lot of day left and he might have to sit here a while before the party broke up. He wanted to learn as much as he could now, while he had the chance. The urge to piss was also creeping into Grid's awareness.

Making another U-turn, Grid drove back out to Orchard and found the nearest convenience store where he pumped a little gas into the Civic so he wouldn't end up stuck somewhere.

In the store he used the toilet, picked out some snacks, a liter bottle of water and two cans of energy drink. That should keep him until the party broke up.

Munching and sipping, Grid kept vigil at the party house. When his head began dropping in nods, he popped open a can of sweetened caffeine concentrate. Just short of three hours later, the first celebrants left the house and drove away. More visitors trickled out over the next hour until only two vehicles remained—a maroon Subaru Outback, and the green VW bug.

Grid was trying to figure out how to piss in the empty water bottle. The car was small and he was big, with little room for activities beyond driving. He looked around. It was dark; getting out and finding a neighborhood bush would be the better choice. Salvation came as Jordan and Red left the house and drove off. Their shadow, Grid, followed three hundred yards behind, expecting the trail to end soon enough that he could hold his bladder.

They returned, as Grid had expected, to the apartment that he assumed they shared. He nodded, satisfied, and drove past and on toward his fraternity.

Around ten thirty Sunday morning, that quiet period before the hung-over frat brothers got up, but after the church-going brothers had gone, Grid left the frat house. He had convinced Shawn that he, Grid, had greater need for the Honda Civic than Shawn had. So he went to a quick-stop, bought snacks and drinks, and got cash back on his debit-card. He stopped at the handful of thrift stores around town, but found them all closed for the Sabbath. Pawn shops came next, and he found what he wanted in the second one—a sturdy aluminum softball bat. He paid cash.

Back at the fraternity, in the car, he wrapped the bat in his jacket, then walked into the house and straight down to the basement. There was an old furnace room that had been relegated to storage after the coal furnace was made obsolete by a heat-pump that stood on a pad outside. The room held a wide variety of crap abandoned by students and stacked in boxes or piled against the wall. The fire marshal would have had a heart attack. Grid dug through boxes of musty clothes until he found a complete outfit large enough to fit over his own. It took quite a search to find a rotting pair of athletic shoes that would fit. There was also a hideous stocking cap and mis-matching gloves, both left handed. Kicking stuff aside, looking for a bag of some kind to hold the clothes and the bat, he spotted another bat leaning in the corner.

"Shit," he said to himself. "I risked buying one when this was already here."

He froze. Digging out his wallet he checked the receipt from the pawn shop. Dammit! Softball bat, aluminum, twelve dollars. They have a record.

Grid looked again at the bat in the corner. Hardball bat, wood, free. It was slightly curved from unknown years of leaning in a damp environment, but it would work. It didn't have to look nice or drive a ball over the fence. He unrolled his jacket, leaned the aluminum one against the wall and lay the wooden replacement on his collection of clothes. Further search found a duffel bag just long enough for the bat.

The duffel looked suspicious with only one set of clothes swelling the middle and a stiff stick holding it nearly rigid, a lot like his coat had. So he gathered more clothes randomly and stuffed them around the bat, with his selected garments crammed in one end to find easily later.

Shawn was getting pissy about his car. Rather than make him mad enough to later remember the loan, Grid drove to a gas station, filled the tank, parked behind the frat house, returned

Shawn's keys and thanked him. The duffel lay snugly in the back of Grid's tiny closet. Nobody would room with him because of his spiky attitude, and that was just fine with him. It meant now that nobody would ask him annoying questions. He looked out his window onto the street and saw that Will's sporty, red, short-bed truck was parked there. Will and he got along pretty well because Will was also on the football team. Will had no plans to go out Sunday evening so he didn't mind loaning Grid his truck.

By seven thirty the house had quieted, with everybody settled in to watch TV or chatting in the common room, or working on homework, or just cruising the web in their rooms. The dorm rats and independents, who made extra cash by mucking out the dining room and kitchen, had gone. Grid put on his jacket, dug the duffel out of the closet and left the house. Somebody in the common room ribbed him about moving out mid-term, but he ignored them.

There was a nice dark alley not far from the frat house where he parked long enough to pull the old clothes on over his own. "God these stink," he muttered. "Should have washed them."

He drove to the apartment shared by Red and Jordan and cruised slowly through the parking lot looking for the green Volkswagen. It was not there. He drove back out and around the block to where he had parked before to watch for its arrival. By eight-forty-five he decided that tonight would not be the night and started the engine.

He made the few corners out but, as he sat waiting to turn onto Orchard, a hunch made him turn east toward the other side of town rather than west toward the frat house. He rolled past the old house where the boat party had been the day before. There, in the driveway, alone, sat the VW bug. Perfect.

Free Body Diagram

Forty minutes later Grid Deimos stepped out the back door and walked away down the dark alley, stopping long enough to strip off the blood-spattered outer clothes and bag them in plastic. He found his shoes that he'd stashed in a bush earlier, put them on and continued to the street, turned right and walked to the truck.

Driving west on Orchard, he had a sudden inspiration and swung by the apartment that he had thought Red and Jordan shared. They didn't, he now knew. He threw the bloodied, bagged clothes into the apartments' dumpster.

He parked on a back street abutting Riverbend Park and walked through the sparse, darkened trees to the shadowed side of the boat shed away from the parking lot, with the weapon wrapped in a light shirt from his basement duffel. A security light illuminated the shed doors, so he stayed close to the dark sidewall, reached around the corner and leaned the gory baseball bat and it's old shirt wrap against the nearest door panel. He knew the other members of the vigilante mob that had humiliated him were certainly rowers, though he couldn't know which ones. This would give them something to think about.

Which gave him something to consider and regret. The way he had left Red arranged might prompt the vigilantes to think of him. Maybe he had gone too far. The statement he had needed to make wouldn't be worth getting caught. They could go to the police, or they might jump him again themselves. He would have to keep an eye over his shoulder.

"Open your mouth please, sir."

Jordan opened his mouth and the lab tech reached in with a long swab, rubbing and rolling it against the inside of his cheek. She dropped it into a tube and capped it.

"Thank you," she said and left.

Jordan was mildly curious about the extent and quality of the their lab, but lacked the inner strength to ask.

The officer across the desk said, "Where were you between eight and ten pm on Sunday?"

"My apartment."

"Alone?"

"Yes."

The policeman glanced at the far away desk where another officer, a woman, interviewed Heidi.

Jordan looked the same direction. Heidi seemed to be in shock. Poor Heidi, he thought. She has been through so much. This last bit really is excessive.

Jord turned back to the officer. "Yes," he said again, dully. "I was alone. You already know where Heidi was and you're hoping I'll claim we were together. I was alone. And I don't have a clue where Heidi was."

The cop rattled the keyboard, making notes, then slid the mouse over to mark a check-box.

"How long have you known the victim?"

"I met her in late August, but didn't get to know her until late September."

"Five months," the officer muttered as he typed into the form. "What was your relationship to her?"

"We collaborated on a new boat for her rowing teams."

"What else?"

"Dance partners. Lovers. Soul mates."

"But you didn't live together?"

Jordan sighed, "She liked her own space."

"Did you resent that?"

"Regretted, not resented."

"Were you jealous of the ex-boyfriend?"

"Tony? Some. He wouldn't turn loose when she made it clear he was done. And she was too polite to tell him to find a motel when he dropped in. But she said there was nothing. I believed her."

The phone on the desk rang and the cop picked it up. "Yeah? You sure? Maybe the state investigator will find something. Just lock it up, tape it, and we'll call him in."

He put the phone down. To Jordan, who still sat with his arms behind the back of his chair in handcuffs, he said, "There's nothing unexpected in your apartment, but we're not done looking."

Jordan shrugged.

"Did you find the bat at her house, or take it with you?" the policeman asked.

"Bat? He used a bat?"

"Why do you say 'he'? What makes you think it wasn't a woman?"

"Catherine...was, a big, strong woman, one-hundred-forty pounds, in peak condition. I doubt that even a man could..." He closed his eyes and paused, "...kill her easy."

"You're a good sized guy," the policeman pointed out.

"I told you. I could never hurt her."

The phone rang again. "Yeah?" The officer listened absently, then his face turned stony and he glared at Jordan.

"Okay," he said in the phone. "Bag it, bring it in and we'll get it to the state lab. Thanks." He hung up.

"What size shoe do you wear?" he asked Jordan.

"Twelve."

The policeman's glare sharpened.

Jordan realized it was time. "May I make a phone call?"

Still glaring, the cop pushed the phone across the desk. Jordan shook his head. "No. I don't know his number. It's programmed into my cell."

The policeman opened his desk drawer and set the smart-phone on the desk in front of Jordan.

"Cuffs?" Jordan asked.

The officer gestured to a big man that had been leaning against a wall behind Jordan through the interview. He released the left wrist but fastened the open cuff to the back chair leg. Winslow looked down and saw that the chair was bolted to the floor.

Jord called James and asked him to find an attorney and, just in case, a bail bondsman.

Since he was done answering questions they escorted Winslow to a back room, strip searched him, sent him through a delousing shower, and handed him paper underwear and a faded orange shirt with pants that rode too low on his hips but cut into his crotch. His clothes were bagged to go to the lab. More deeply depressed than ever, he stepped into the jail cell.

There were no discrepancies between Jordan's and Heidi's answers beyond the minor differences common to any human accounts. The police, on the off-chance that Jordan was not the killer, suggested that Heidi find a place away from her apartment to stay for the next week.

"Why?" Heidi asked.

The friendly officer said, "The murder weapon was found at the boat shed. We figure this all has to be related to the rowing. That puts you and your teammates at risk. We've warned them. They're spreading out. Please be careful about your contacts. Is there someplace you could stay that is not associated with rowing?"

Heidi considered for a moment. "I think Jennifer, an old basketball friend, might put me up."

"Give her a call and we'll drive you over."

Heidi looked to where Jordan had been interviewed. "Where's Mr. Winslow?"

"Let me check." The officer punched an internal number. "Did you turn Winslow loose? Oh. Okay. Thanks." She hung up.

To Heidi she said, "He's in a cell."

"Why? Can I see him?"

"There are some loose ends that can't be addressed until the state lab processes the evidence. He'll have to stay until they get back to us. Two or three days usually. You can come in during visiting hours tomorrow."

Monday, the night Heidi had spent at Jordan's, at ten-fifteen pm, as Grid had watched Heidi's apartment from the shadows of the same grove where they'd had rough love, the police arrived. Grid had faded away and walked back to the frat.

The light in the jail cell went dark at ten o'clock. Jordan had taken the last of the twelve bunks and lay on it, stunned. So this is our justice system. Light from the hall still illuminated most of the cell, but there were dim portions where prisoners could at least hope for sleep without glare. Jordan discovered why his bunk was the last taken. The sharp bulb in the hallway ceiling shined directly into his eyes. He rolled away.

The constant odor of vomit, urine, shit and armpit grew more intense and Jordan felt the disturbance of air through the short hairs of his neck. He rolled half toward the motion and a man knelt there closely silhouetted beside his bunk.

"I can kill all of you. Any time I want." The silhouette rasped. "Kill you all. Anytime." His horrible breath overcame the cell's ambient effluvium.

"Fine," Jord said. "Get some sleep and we'll do a head count in the morning." He rolled back toward the wall.

"Anytime," the voice said, fading toward his own bunk.

Jordan lay for a long time listening to the harsh echoes of the jail—coughing, farting, moaning, sharp calls, sudden arguments, yips of imagined, dreamed or real distress, the splash of urine into the stainless toilet, and then the biting, disturbing odor briefly overcoming the staler scents. The ungodly loud flush. His eyes were crisp with exhaustion, but he could not sleep. He tried following a whispered, Spanish conversation in the next cell. The talk and the random sounds seemed to be falling into a rhythmic pattern, he began to inject meaning in the conversation, though he didn't speak the language, and he felt his sense fading. An uproar rattled down the hallway as another prisoner was led to a cell. This noise agitated the whole jail, which took time to settle again. When the rhythms returned he plunged deep into sleep and later arrivals went unnoticed. He dreamed horrible dreams, his whimpers joining the night misery symphony.

Tuesday night, with Jordan in jail and Heidi disappeared, Grid strolled by Jordan's apartment. He saw the yellow warning tape across the door. There were no police cars parked in the neighborhood. It was unlikely that this low-rent housing would bother with security cameras. He leaned patiently in a shadow across the street for two hours, watching. Nothing happened.

He approached the apartment obliquely, sidled up to one of the windows and jammed a long screwdriver into the lower corner of the frame and another at the top. The lower corner of the pane made a crisp crunching sound, but the cheap plastic latch gave before the glass and the pane slid open.

Grid was looking for something that would lead him to Heidi, or the other bitches who had shamed him. This he did not find, but he knew he was on the right track when he discovered a copy of the newspaper article about his fall down the fraternity steps. Jordan was in on it.

Wednesday an attorney showed up and requested a meeting with Jordan. They met in a small consultation room. "Mr. Winslow, I'm Roger Menken. James DeWitt gave me a retainer to act on your behalf."

"How much?"

"Don't worry about that now. Worry about your situation. My understanding is that you are a suspect in the murder of your girlfriend, ah," he glanced at his notes, "Catherine Sinjohn. Right now it doesn't look good, but all the evidence is circumstantial and, unless they can tie you directly to the clothes and the bat, they won't be able to convict you."

"I didn't do it."

"Good. That'll make the defense easier."

"And what clothes?"

"Of course. They wouldn't tell you. A garbage bag of bloody clothes was found in the dumpster at your apartment. Since there has been no other crime lately to explain them, it has to be what Catherine's killer wore. Very coincidental that they turned up at your place, and the cops are going to make the most of that. Apparently the shoe size matches yours. You should not have volunteered that."

Jordan glanced at his jail slippers. "They would have known by now anyway."

"True. But no more voluntary remarks unless I okay them. Now, tell me every minute of your life from Saturday afternoon up to and including your arrest on Tuesday."

The attorney asked him questions to clarify and fill in gaps. There was nothing to be done about the alibi, or lack of alibi, for the time of the murder, but the prosecutors would have to prove Jordan had been at the scene.

After an hour Roger, satisfied that he had everything, went to the door and signaled an officer. The state investigator, Wallace Rasmussen, the lone detective in a corner office of the local state patrol building, joined them in the little room and asked Jordan the same questions that Roger had.

"Okay," the detective said. "Now walk me through the weekend again. Slowly."

When Jordan got to the part about fixing an evening meal to break from correcting papers the detective interrupted. "And you used that break to go see Ms Sinjohn. You argued about the ex-boyfriend that had spent the previous two nights there. You brought the bat with you to show her who the boss was and that you were serious. The argument got out of hand and you killed her. When you realized what you'd done, you went home, changed out of the killing clothes and threw them away."

"No. I ate and went back to correcting papers."

"Why did you arrange the body the way you did? Trying to send a message to Tony?"

"Arranged? What do you mean arranged?" Jordan asked.

"You were showing why you killed her and letting Tony know."

"I don't know what you're talking about. Why isn't Tony here answering questions? He's the one at the house."

"Tony's credit card was used to buy gas in Pocatello within two hours of the murder. He couldn't have been anywhere near Evansville."

Jordan thought a moment. "He could have planned to do it before he came, and had a friend hold his card. A quick call and the friend would run out and get gas."

"Nice scenario, but he also turned up at the ski lodge for work, with his car, the next morning. Not feasible if he was killing Ms Sinjohn at nine o'clock Sunday night."

The interrogation lasted for two hours.

Jordan returned to the lockup where he was reminded that all lives in the cell could be taken at any time by the very odorous cell-mate. Even if Jordan had been less withdrawn, he would not have taken the poor man any more seriously than the other indifferent prisoners had.

The state investigator joined the local officers in their conference room. "I don't think he's the guy. You'll want to hold him 'til the lab reports show up, but I wager none of it will connect him to the murder."

The chief said, "We had the same feeling. His story is consistent, and the jealousy motive is too slim. I mean, the ex-boyfriend was gone. Everybody we interviewed said the victim was committed to Winslow and finished with the ex. And he really did have papers to correct the evening of the murder. But if it wasn't him, who did kill the woman?"

They sat silently in thought.

Rasmussen said, "Winslow had an interesting take on the ex-boyfriend's alibi. Suggested Tony had a friend run the credit card in Pocatello. I know," he said at their expressions. "Improbable. And it supposes that he planned murder before he even left Colorado. It's more likely he believed he could get the woman back and only planned murder after he found out he couldn't. Same jealousy motive, just the other way 'round. He killed her because Winslow had cut in. Some of the woman's friends suggested he was pissed. Of course we have to explain how he and his car could have made it to work less than eleven hours after the deed. I've made that drive. It's sixteen to eighteen hours in summer. More in winter. At best he would only have about four hours sleep before work."

"He hired somebody to kill her," one of the cops said.

"Possible, but in a two day stay? Not much time to find a reliable contract killer. His finances fall short. Maybe in these modern times hit-men are taking Master Card, but I doubt it."

The chief said, "The violence of that broom handle violation has to mean a sexual motive. We've been thinking it's related to the rowing because the murder weapon was found at the boat shed, but whoever impaled that poor woman had a powerful, sick, sexual motive. Preliminaries from the autopsy say if she hadn't already been dead, it would have killed her. Penetrated through the vaginal wall into the abdominal cavity.

She would have bled out before she was found. Sexual revenge points the finger at a frustrated ex-boyfriend."

"Okay," the state man said. "The old boyfriend has the best motive. But his alibi is unbreakable."

One of the cops said, "Airplanes."

"How did he get his car to Vail?" the chief asked.

"Like Winslow suggested. He had a buddy help him."

"But," Rasmussen said, "if he knew the alibi value of a credit card record in Pocatello, he would know the danger of a credit and ID trail left by flying."

"A look-alike?" the first cop guessed. "Say he had a friend that lived somewhere along the drive. Maybe Boise. Say the friend and he look enough alike to pass on each other's ID. They meet, swap credit cards and ID. Tony grabs a flight out of Boise to Evansville. The buddy keeps driving toward Vail, stopping for gas in Pocatello. Tony kills his ex-girlfriend, grabs a flight to Vail. They meet again, swap cards and the accomplice flies home to Boise."

"Damn!" the chief said. "That would work. Unlikely, but workable. Okay people, split up the airlines and start calling. Look for anybody with that flight pattern for those dates. And remember, they could have started at Pocatello, Twin Falls, Boise or any closer airport. In fact, the first point could be anywhere in a two hour radius around Evansville, including Evansville itself."

His team groaned at the scope of the task.

"Get everybody on it," the chief said. He turned to the state guy. "Will you chip in?"

"Sure, give me a slice of the pie, but I want to question Winslow one more time. If it wasn't him and wasn't Tony, maybe he has some clue who the killer is. In the meantime, we'll still want to keep him 'til the lab is done. Judges are pretty relaxed about material witness rules since 9/11. Holding him shouldn't be a problem. When the lab report shows up, before letting him go, get the prosecutor to depose Winslow in case we lose him before this comes to the grand jury."

"You going to tell him about the postmortem broom handle rape?"

"No. That's the only unpublicized detail we have to ID the perpetrator."

Catherine's assistant coach had gone to the coach's house around nine-thirty Monday morning when Coach didn't show at the school. She tried the locked front door and then went around from window to window until she saw a spray of red hair on the floor, surrounded by a spray of red blood. She called 911 from the spot and refused to look again into the window. She had no notion of the disposition of the room and the body. Nobody outside the police department, and the murderer, knew the detail of the broom.

Jordan's shocked condition did not allow much creative speculation about potential killers for the state detective. Catherine was a strong-willed woman who did not suffer fools, but everybody liked her. Regarding the rowing, and the boat, the only one he could think of who was the least unhappy was Professor Durning, but he was fifty-seven and overweight, probably beyond his days of swinging a bat with effect, and he had grudgingly grown to accept the project.

Were there any other jealous lovers in the mix?

No, nobody came to mind.

Free Body Diagram

Heidi arrived at the jail an hour after Jordan's second interview with the state detective. They sat glumly. She asked, "Any idea when they'll let you go?"

"After the lab results, I guess. How have you been?"

"Struggling. They told me not to go back to my place. Dropped in long enough to get some of my stuff and went to Jennifer's. Is jail awful?"

"Not too bad. I didn't like the strip search, and I don't like the smell, and I don't like the noise, and I don't like the guy that keeps threatening to kill us all. And I haven't taken a shit because the stainless toilet, with no seat, sits open to the world. That's beginning to distress me. But, no. It's not awful." He smiled.

Heidi smiled back sadly. "Not awful. Good."

She looked away from his eyes and said, "I quit the sculling team."

Jordan didn't ask why. He knew why. She had too much of the world weighing her down and needed to toss out cargo to stay afloat. He also knew that he should encourage her to soldier on, but who was he, a man verging on suicide, to tell her that?

"It'll free up a lot of time," he said. "And you don't have to come here to see me."

"Yes I do. We're tied together by everything that's happened. It would be wrong to leave you on your own, and I still need your support. We, you and me, are a free body diagram, like in dynamics. We proceed together by acting as a single, isolated unit. Without that, nothing can make sense."

Jordan just nodded.

Heidi said, "My parents called. The story hit national news and they made the connection between coach and me. Tried to get me to come home, but I convinced them I'm fine. Lying gets easier with practice."

They sat still.

Jordan said, "I'll call you when I get out. Will you come tomorrow?"

"Of course. See you then."

A memorial was held on Saturday at the funeral home, which had done its best for Catherine. It was a closed casket ceremony because their best was not adequate and no funerary artist could have done her justice.

Jordan petitioned for, and was granted, a leave from jail to attend. He was accompanied by two burly officers in suits and wore an ill-fitting loaner another cop had brought in for him. He sat through the ceremony torn between a desire to stand up and scream, or to faint. He compromised by posing like a stone man with tears creeping down his face. After the memorial Catherine's body was taken to the airport and transported to Florida to be interred by her family.

The turnaround at the state lab was abysmal, so Jordan remained in jail until Monday, when the reports arrived indicating no connecting evidence at his apartment, and not a hint of his DNA on the spattered clothes, or the shoes. Naturally he had left some at Catherine's house, the murder scene, but nothing relevant to the crime. His semen had turned up in the autopsy of the victim, but had obviously been there too long to coincide with the murder. Unfortunately there was also no evidence of the actual murderer on the bloodied clothes beyond three short hairs, without follicles, found in the ugly stocking cap. They did find spores of three types of fungi that permeated the clothing and which are typically found in old, unwashed clothing stored in a damp environment. This did not suggest anything useful, though the bat had the same spores and therefore was assumed to come from the same place.

"I recommend," the releasing officer said to Jordan, "that you do not contact Ms van Vleet. Nothing prevents you, but it could put you both at risk. There was evidence of a break-in at your apartment after we sealed it. We have to assume it's connected to the murder. I also suggest that you find someplace else to stay for a while for your safety."

"Can you give me a lift?"

"Sorry, sir. We can call a taxi."

"Don't bother. I'll walk."

It was about three miles to his apartment, just a good stretch of his long legs. The clothes he wore were those he'd worn at his arrest, screened for every bit of evidence they might hold, then laundered in cheap industrial detergent and returned to him. They smelled funny and were oddly stiff and crisp. He looked forward to getting a change, but he was disappointed. His home was a mess and all of his clothes had been confiscated for evidence, but not returned.

Jordan went through the stale apartment methodically, looking for important stuff. His computer was gone. He figured that whoever broke in had taken it until he remembered setting it down on the curb in front of general engineering before putting Heidi in the taxi. Gone forever, he guessed. At least the backup drive holding his thesis software still lay in the drawer where he had left it, though shifted out of position by somebody. He checked the window that had been the entry point for the break-in. It would never latch again on its own. Not like it would give any security even if it could latch, and what difference did that make?

The search through his papers left him unsatisfied. He knew that several items would have been lost in his abandoned New Yorker bag, but something nagged at the back of his mind.

Jordan called Heidi to let her know that he had been released from jail. They arranged to meet the next day for lunch.

Replacing all of his clothes was not as simple as it seemed. He had never bought everything at once before and it put a shocking dent in his savings account. There was a Walmart in hiking distance where he picked up a selection of the cheapest clothes he could find, including a lined, hooded windbreaker and insulated gloves so he could ride his ancient Schwinn Varsity bicycle through the cold winter air to more distant stores. He deplored shopping at Walmart, but he also deplored the necessity for him and others with limited funds to be forced to either shop there or go without.

He found a used laptop at a pawn shop and loaded his work into it from the backup drive. If that backup had been stolen during the break-in or confiscated for evidence by the police, there was another locked in his desk at the campus office. He, like Heidi, felt too burdened to continue beyond that, so the work of his master's project stalled, and, though he knew he should get back into the teaching, he begged Dave and James to carry him one more week. They agreed without hesitation.

Grid Deimos split his time among scholastic demands, sports conditioning, and watching the apartments of Heidi and Jordan. The two people he stalked had dropped from sight. Heidi didn't show at the boat shed anymore and Jordan seemed to have vanished completely, most likely to jail because of the clever trick of the bloody clothes in Jordan's dumpster. It was inconvenient for Grid to cover all of his bases on foot, but he couldn't continue borrowing cars from frat brothers, nor could he afford his own. His scholarship barely covered the costs of school and his parents were poor as church bats in a belfry.

By chance, late Tuesday morning Grid was just arriving to stake out Jordan's apartment and noticing the yellow tape was gone, when Winslow left the building with a pack on his back. Grid knew Jordan didn't have a car and was ready to follow him wherever he went until the bastard pulled a rickety road bike out of a storage shed and peddled away at a rate that Grid couldn't match on foot. At least Grid had discovered that Jordan was out of jail and still in town.

Heidi and Jordan met at The Sub-burgs, where the gimmick was burgers served on hoagie buns. The decor was plastered in images of ranch-style neighborhood houses with children playing on finely groomed lawns that also had Black Angus cattle grazing upon them. Heidi was horrified.

"They have a bean burger that's okay," Jordan said.

After they ordered, Jordan said, "I think the police are on the wrong track. Even though Tony was more upset than anybody expected about the break-up, he's not the type to commit to *any* project. Murder included. But I have lived in such a fog since.... I couldn't help the police with anything that might lead to the killer."

The police had, by then, already exonerated Tony because of three factors: His phone history did not include contact with anyone in a position to help him with the plan, no combination of flight schedules could have made the necessary connections, and he had visited a woman in Tremonton who would not have been fooled by an impostor.

Heidi looked uncertain. She asked, "Did the police say to move out of your apartment?"

"Yes."

"It might be a good idea. If Tony didn't do it, then somebody dangerous is still out there. And it doesn't matter whether the connection is rowing, you'd be a target."

He shrugged but looked away from her eyes.

"Oh, Jord. Don't. You helped me through my trouble. I need you again to handle Coach's death. Even if you don't care about yourself, please be careful for me."

He smiled lightly. "Leverage, eh? Okay, I'll get a motel room and hope the cops catch the bastard before he finds me."

She studied him. "Good. Coach wouldn't want you hurt for her sake either."

Jordan could see she was struggling with something else. She had been growing more agitated since they arrived at The Sub-burgs.

"What's bothering you?" He asked.

"I've done a lot of thinking this last week. I'm reluctant to bring it up, but we might be at more risk if I don't tell you."

"If you can help catch the monster that killed Catherine, you have to tell the police."

"It's complicated. I don't want to go to the police, but you have to know. Coach trusted you. So she might have told you." She paused and Jordan began to suspect what was coming. "You know the guy who hurt me? Coach took some of the crew out and taught him a lesson. A very nasty lesson. Knowing what that guy is like, imagine what he would do if he figured out that it was Coach who did it to him."

"Gerard Deimos," Jordan said.

"She told you his name?"

"No. I researched it after she told me what they did to him. If I hadn't been so distracted... Shit! That's what was missing from my apartment! I printed that article. It was gone after the break-in."

"It's him, then," Heidi whispered. "That monster. It's him. Nobody else would be interested in the article."

A killer was stalking them and—they thought back over the last week—had probably just missed finding them through pure chance. They stared at each other. They both looked around at the other diners. Heidi saw that Deimos was not there. Jordan didn't know what he looked like, so he assessed every male for the age and physique that might mark the mad football tackle.

"We have to tell the police." Jordan said.

"Wait, wait, wait," Heidi said with calming gestures. "If we tell them, the whole story will come out. The fact that I didn't report it. My family will hear."

"Heidi, I don't want to put you through more pain, but this guy murdered Catherine. Turn him in."

She looked at him strangely. Then she relaxed. It was Catherine he was thinking about, and it was her, Heidi, too. If that madman wasn't put away she, and Jordan, would be in danger, but they weren't the only consideration.

Heidi asked, "Did Coach tell you who helped her with Deimos?"

"No."

"Me neither. But the police will want to know. Then it will be them on trial for assault and rape. Even though you know the guy deserved it."

Jordan was rolling all of this in his mind. "There's also my vow, though it doesn't amount to a hill of beans beside the rest. I swore that I'd never tell what she did. This late in the game we'd also be considered accessories in the assault on Deimos."

Heidi asked, "Did Coach tell you about the other victims? The other women Deimos raped?"

He shook his head.

"You'll be proud of her. She would have taken care of the guy anyway for my sake, but she wanted to know whether it was a one-off assault or habitual behavior. So she set up a research program. It was genius. She made an anonymous rape report chart that included the pictures of five men and a line of check-boxes under each. At the top it said, 'If you have been raped by one of these men, place a mark in a box under his picture.' She printed a hundred of them and stuck them in women's toilets all over town. She took four of the pictures off the web and altered them so they were not likenesses. Only Deimos' picture was real. When she collected the forms there were thirty-seven marks under Deimos. There were twelve marks, total, on the other men. She assumed that the other men were false positives, and that Deimos probably got duplicate marks by some women, but it was obvious that I was not his first victim. He had it coming and she proved it."

Jordan said, "She was..."

"Yes she was," Heidi said.

Their elongated hamburgers arrived.

Neither knew where to take the conversation after these revelations, so they ate quietly, but kept casting looks at the door with every arrival, and studying the sidewalks outside.

"What do we do?" Heidi asked.

"Keep a low profile."

"How? We have classes. He knows I'm studying engineering. All he has to do is wait."

"But he won't be able to do anything in public."

"I can't have him follow me back to Jennifer's. She'd be in danger."

Jordan was thinking it, but it was Heidi who voiced it. "We have to take him out first."

"That," he said slowly, "would be hard. It has to be just us. You and me. The Free Body Diagram. We can't recruit anybody else. And he's paranoid. Hyper-vigilant. Dangerous. He can't be surprised again."

"It'll take planning."

"Without any time." They glanced at the window.

Heidi said, "If only I had turned him in. Coach would be alive."

"You didn't start this, Heidi. It was him. Nobody made him attack you. Nobody made him kill Catherine. He could have reported the vigilantes, just like you had the option of reporting the rape, and maybe she would be in jail, but she wouldn't be dead. Of course, he'd be in jail, too."

"You think the police will connect him?"

"How could they? Without the big pieces of the puzzle, your injuries and Catherine's justice, nothing points to him."

She thought for a time. "Maybe we could tie him to the evidence somehow. The clothes or the weapon, and let the police take over."

"That's as dangerous as just taking care of him ourselves, and no matter how it becomes public, you and the vigilante women will be exposed."

They nibbled a while at the unappetizing hoagie-burgers, made less palatable by the mood.

"We can't do it," Heidi said.

"Of course not. It would make us monsters, too."

"Then what?"

"How 'bout this? I'll report him to the police, no names. Base my suspicions only on what Catherine told me. I can leave you out of it. I can leave the vigilantes out of it and tell it as if she did it alone. She had the strength. And the rape victim poll would give her the justification if a rumor set her off."

Heidi pushed the uneaten half of her Sub-burger away and swallowed a rinsing mouthful of lemon-water. "Might work."

"But first, I have to get out of the apartment before he shows up again."

That afternoon Jordan collected his toiletries, the books and papers related to his thesis, his new computer, and the backup drive, tossing them into his day-pack. He would come back with a taxi for the rest after he'd found new accommodation.

Along the old route of state highway four, on the east side of Evansville, a strip of low budget motels struggled to survive the loss of tourist traffic which had resulted from construction of the freeway bypass. They all rented rooms at daily, weekly or monthly rates. Jordan took a week, to start, at the Rebates Motel, stowed his stuff and called a taxi.

Jordan was sure the police still considered him a person of interest, and were tracking him with the GPS in his smart phone, so he bought two throw-away cell phones. These would allow him and Heidi to move around without police knowledge. If they spent time together against the wishes of the police the next theory would surely be that Jordan and Heidi themselves had conspired to murder Catherine.

As an afterthought he had the taxi driver swing by the Rugged Outfitter and Surplus store and bought four grizzly bear pepper spray canisters displayed in blister packs with bear-bells included. These were located significantly beside the pocket tasers, of which he also bought two.

In the evening Jordan checked the strobe lights on his bicycle and rode over to Jennifer's.

The door opened on another tall, strong woman. Jordan, surrounded lately by scullers and basketball players, was beginning to forget that most women were less statuesque.

To her puzzled look he said, "Hi. I'm looking for Heidi? I'm Jordan."

Jennifer beamed a smile. "At last!" she said. "I get to meet the incredible Mr. Winslow."

She reached forward to shake his hand while he grinned sheepishly and said, "Just Jordan."

"Come on in, Just-Jordan. Heidi!" she shouted over her shoulder. "Your elderly friend is here!"

As they came into the living room Heidi peeked curiously out of the kitchen. She smiled. "Hi," she said. "Sit. You want tea?"

"Sure, thanks."

"Green, right?"

"Yes." But he did not sit down. Instead he went to lean in the kitchen doorway while she prepped the teapot.

Heidi said, "I thought you'd call before you came over."

"I've been thinking about that," he said. "The police are likely tracking our phones. Here," he said reaching into a pocket for a throw-away cell. "This is for you. I have another. My number is programmed into yours, and yours in mine. This way we can keep in touch privately. We can leave the smart phones at home whenever we meet."

Jennifer said. "Intrigue! I love it!"

Jordan chuckled. "When you put it like that it sounds crazy. But circumstances are serious enough... " He shrugged.

Jennifer looked abashed. "Oh," she said. "Sorry. I wasn't thinking."

"Don't worry. Maybe humor is what we need right now. I brought these, too," he said, handing Heidi two pepper sprays and a taser.

"Like mine!" she said and pulled the same brand of spray out of a waist clip.

"Cool. But keep one for a spare and give the other to Jennifer. In future, Jennifer, answer the door with that in your hand, ready to go. You know what Grid Deimos looks like?"

She nodded.

"If he shows up, don't hesitate. Blind him. If you can close the door, lock it. If he gets in, zap him with a taser, get Heidi, leave fast and call 911."

"My God," Jennifer said. "It is serious, isn't it." She took the other spray and frowned absently at it.

They each stood quietly in their own thoughts until the kettle whistled and Heidi filled the teapot.

"Let's sit at the table," Heidi said, moving the teapot to the center of the dining table.   Jordan sat down as Jennifer grabbed cups.

While the tea steeped, they sat uncomfortably.

Jordan asked, "How's the new boat?"

"The crews love it." Heidi said. "They've done even better than the six second gain. We might really have a winning season, finally."

Heidi poured the tea.

Jordan said, "I'm taking one more week off. James and Dave have been great. What do you study, Jennifer?"

They chatted until the pot was empty and Jordan stood. "I wanted to deliver that phone and stuff. I'll talk to the cops tomorrow morning. Then call to let you know how it went. Jennifer, thanks for the hospitality; it's nice to meet you."

They ushered him to the door and sent him on his way.

"He's kind of cute, for an old guy," Jennifer said.

Deimos realized that both Jordan and Heidi had relocated. He would have to try other channels to get back on their track. He remembered that Heidi was studying engineering, though he didn't know which variety, so the engineering college provided the best chance at reestablishing contact with her, and Jordan almost certainly must be associated with the school, too. He would find them again. And she would pay for blabbing. And Jordan? He was probably in on it from the beginning, might even have been one of the attackers; Grid couldn't be sure that they were really all women since it had been dark and only Red had spoken.

In the meantime he reengaged with his fraternity. His behavior had improved over the last few days and the brothers were gratefully welcoming him into their center in the usual male fashion—by heaping ridicule on him. It was fortunate that they did not know the source of his calm, or they would have emptied the house in panic. He had killed. He got away with it, and he was putting on a performance to show his normalcy, his ordinariness. The police could never suspect a good frat boy like him of the horrendous pulping death he had delivered to that fucking bitch. And the broom handle revenge. She slid two feet across the floor before the wall stopped her so he could shove the handle in far enough to satisfy. It had given suddenly and he knew he was home.

"So," Rasmussen, the state investigator, said as he sat down behind the desk across from Jordan, "you thought of somebody."

Jordan passed the detective a newly printed copy of the article about Grid's tumble on the stair, along with a picture of Deimos that he had downloaded and cropped from the school yearbook photo of last year's football team.

Rasmussen read the short blurb and studied the picture. He looked up. "Where's the connection? Where's the motive?"

"That wasn't a fall that kept him from playing. It was Catherine."

"How so? Broken heart?"

"Broken bones. She took him by surprise and beat the hell out of him."

Officers loitering in the station drifted into hearing range.

"Why and how?"

"She heard rumors that Deimos was assaulting women. To test it she organized an anonymous poll and posted it in women's toilets. It proved that he had raped several. She took him down that night," he gestured at the article, "with a taser, trussed him with zip-ties and lectured him about gentlemanly behavior while she beat the shit out of him with a wrapped pipe club. To make the lesson memorable and graphic, she jammed a broomstick up his ass."

Rasmussen's eyebrows raised and he exchanged glances with an officer over Jordan's shoulder.

"You have my attention. How did you find this out?"

"She told me during a drunken exchange of secrets."

"You had knowledge of assault and battery, and rape, of this Deimos guy, by your girlfriend, but you didn't tell the police. That's a crime."

"So is what he was doing."

"Then she or his victims should have reported him."

"He didn't report being attacked," Jordan pointed out. "You think it's easier for a woman to come forward?"

"We're talking about your crime of accessory. But I'm more interested in the murder we're trying to solve. If Deimos did it, why did he wait this long?"

"I assume he was healing, and probably just recently stumbled onto Catherine's identity."

"And what made *you* suddenly think of *him*?"

"Did the police collect a copy of that news article from my apartment for evidence?"

Rasmussen turned to the computer, pulled up the file, and ran a search of the evidence log. "No," he said.

"I didn't think so. I printed that article when Catherine told me the story. It was on my desk at the apartment, but was missing after the break-in. Who else would have taken only that? If I wasn't in shock, I might have thought of him before you let me out of jail."

Rasmussen studied Winslow while considering all of this, absently tapping a pen on the desk. He turned toward the city police chief. "Can we talk in your office?"

Once there he said, "I think you should get a warrant to pull in this Deimos, and search his fraternity. It all ties together too well to be bullshit. Especially the broomstick. Winslow could only include that if he killed Sinjohn himself, and I still don't think he did. He's not telling us everything, but we've got the relevant material."

They grilled Jordan for another half hour and sent him home. The duty judge signed their warrants when they submitted Jordan's statement along with the central, secret fact of the broom. Then a request was sent to the newspaper for any background material that hadn't made it into the story about Deimos' accident. A search was initiated of his phone records and debit card use. Rasmussen phoned the hospital, faxed them a copy of the warrant and asked for the emergency room reports on Deimos for the night in question. The city records produced a police report filed the next day as a follow-up to the emergency room physician's suspicions. The officer had been as doubtful as the doctor, but could not find anything to justify further investigation, and Deimos had been intractable.

Rasmussen studied the doctor's report. The physician had concluded that the fall on the stair was fiction because there were no lacerations and the injuries were too evenly distributed. Stairs have edges and corners, but the patient displayed only widespread bruising and broken bones. The only cut had been to his tongue. In the notes section the doctor had barely legibly

106

jotted "Beaten? Multiple assailants?" His acuity must have been heightened by the suspicion because he had even mentioned the abrasions on Deimos' wrists that would be accounted for by the zip-tie binding. Everything Jordan had said rang true. If the anal rape had caused damage, either Deimos was able to cover it up (he certainly hadn't told the doctor) or any pain it gave him was hidden by pain from the more obvious injuries. Wallace Rasmussen answered, to himself, the question that Jordan had asked earlier. Yes, he thought it might be easier for a woman to come forward and report rape than for a star football player at the peak of his manhood.

Rasmussen glanced back over the form. "Multiple assailants?" Winslow either didn't know it all or wasn't telling it all. There was also his suspiciously weak excuse of the rumors of rape that had supposedly caught Sinjohn's interest in Grid Deimos originally. Not likely. There must have been something else. And when Rasmussen considered this, the answer was obvious, the corner of the geometry that didn't fit: Heidi van Vleet.

The phallocentric culture in which he and his fellow officers lived had made them all assume that Winslow, Sinjohn and van Vleet occupied a male fantasy triangle of some sort. Either the older pair had co-opted the young woman for tag-team sex, or Winslow was working her as a replacement or supplement to the older woman. None of them had considered the reality, that Winslow and Sinjohn were two caring people acting as surrogate parents to a young woman traumatized by violent rape. No wonder van Vleet was bonded to them both. Rasmussen did not envy these two survivors their future sorting out of the relationship, when they would realize the original need was gone and would either have to be replaced, or the relationship dissolved.

The police chief had a friend in the university administration office, so they sidestepped the warrant and accessed Heidi's attendance record. She had failed to appear in class the whole week just prior to Grid Deimos' accident.

Now that he had a picture of the chain of events, Rasmussen saw it's inevitability, and the certainty that Deimos was the murderer.

Grid returned from afternoon class, walking the route toward his fraternity. He stopped short. Three police cars barricaded the street about a block from his house, and, a block beyond the house on the far side, three more cruisers turned people away.

Grid turned casually around and disappeared.

The search turned up nothing meaningful in Grid's room, but the furnace room was well stocked with musty clothing which, when tested, proved to have the same three fungal spores that had been found on the murder clothes. (Eventually another test of samples vacuumed from Grid's closet turned up the same spores.) Strangely, an aluminum softball bat was discovered and nearly ignored as unrelated until one officer suggested checking it for prints. Based on the predominant fingerprints found in Deimos' room, it was apparent that Grid had handled the bat extensively. A frat brother had seen a bat there months ago but could not swear that it was this bat. The police ran a check of second-hand stores and pawn shops. A pawn broker did have records for a bat matching the description, sold on the day of the murder, but he couldn't remember who bought it.

"It was a college kid. What do I know? They all look the same; too young and too healthy. A bat in February? Why not?

The weather was nice. I recall thinking that the next day I'd get a good steak and have barbecue with the wife for Valentine's Day."

"Was he short? Tall?" the officer asked.

"Tall, I guess. All kids are tall now."

Deimos had used his debit card, the day before the murder, at a Kwik-Stop less than a mile from Catherine Sinjohn's house. He bought snacks and two-point-one gallons of gasoline. They asked around the fraternity and confirmed that Grid did not have a car, but had borrowed one Saturday afternoon and Sunday morning, which the owner remembered clearly because Grid had returned it with thanks and a full tank of gas, completely out of character. Another brother had loaned his pickup Sunday evening, and Grid returned the keys at around nine forty-five. The lab techs vacuumed the truck and turned up a good sample of the three spores from the murder clothes.

The hairs found in the hat microscopically matched hairs collected from Deimos' room but, because there were no roots, a DNA test could not connect them to him.

The evidence was abundant and compelling, but Deimos had surfaced only once, after the police tried to catch him at his residence, withdrawing three hundred dollars from an ATM at a convenience store two miles from his fraternity house while his room was being searched. Then he vanished.

Thursday afternoon Jordan called the police for a progress report.

"No idea," the officer said. "Hard to believe he could disappear so quick without help, so I guess he probably hitched a ride out of town. Where could he be hiding if he hadn't?"

"Did you call his family?"

"Yeah. They haven't heard from him."

"Okay. Thanks."

Saturday afternoon, Heidi called Jordan.

"My roommates have invited us to the old apartment this evening for a small party. A couple of guys they know, you and me, music, burgers on the grill and chips with dip. How 'bout it?"

"Why not. When?"

"Bike over to here at four thirty and we can walk together to the apartment."

"See you then."

They walked by the grocery and picked up a couple of two liter bottles of soda pop, a bag of tortilla chips and three flavors of chip dip. One benefit of living in a semi-arid climate with two large intersecting rivers nearby is soft, pleasant, winter evenings. It was almost possible to forget the recent horrors they had endured, and just enjoy the moment and the company of a trusted friend grown comfortable with time.

Heidi still had her key. She unlocked the door calling, "We're here!", and pushed it open so Jordan, lugging the groceries, could pass through.

Gerard Deimos paused for an instant. He wanted the bitch first, but she was behind the Jordan guy, so he swung at him. The thirty inch long piece of one inch galvanized pipe whistled toward Jordan's head, but Grid's hesitation gave Jordan the instant it took to get past the surprise and raise his arms. The club smashed into the grocery bag, blasting tortilla chips into a cloud, accompanied by a spray of dip, but the tough, plastic soda bottles absorbed most of the energy without damage, saving Jordan's skull. Even so, the pipe kept enough momentum to break his left forearm with a crunching snap. The club pulled back for another swing and Jordan charged directly into Grid's chest with his right shoulder. Grid slammed against the wall and swung the pipe down against Jord's buttocks and thighs, too close to hit better targets. Jordan kept his head down and, pinning the man as best he could, pounded his right fist into Grid's ribs and kicked up with a knee into his groin. Jordan was barely aware that his thighs were numbing from repeated blows of the pipe. Then a spatter of pepper spray bounced into his face, burning his eyes and shutting off his wind. He heard the chatter of a taser beside his right ear and felt a secondary jolt of electricity conducted through the contact between his right temple and Grid's right jaw. Grid twitched. Jordan was grabbed from behind and thrown across the room against the breakfast bar. He heard the crackle of the taser again, followed by a padded ringing of the pipe club landing on the carpet. There was a silent pause while he tried to clear his burning vision or catch a breath of air. A terrible ringing thwock sounded, like the combination of a melon hitting a sidewalk and an ax chopping ice. Then again, and a third, then a fourth time and the floor thundered as Gerard Deimos fell full length on his face, crushing an Ikea coffee table. Jordan's watering eyes began to clear enough to see the shape of the downed man with a vengeful Heidi standing spread-legged above him, every muscle strung like cable, with the pipe raised behind her right shoulder, and a high, barely audible whine breathing out her nose.

"No," Jordan wheezed. "He's down. Leave him. My eyes!"

Heidi threw the pipe against a wall, came to Jordan, took him by the good arm and guided him to the kitchen sink. "Bend down. Put your face sideways under the faucet." She ran it till it was lukewarm, then swung it over his eyes.

Behind them Grid moaned.

"Hold onto the counter," Heidi told Jordan, took his taser from the belt clip and stepped to Deimos, jolting him in the neck with the fully charged weapon.

"You okay for a minute?" she asked Jordan.

"Yeah."

She went into the nearest bedroom where she found her two roommates, well but bound back-to-back on the bed with duct tape. She walked back to the living room for scissors from the desk drawer, returned to the bedroom and released them enough so they could finish removing the tape. Giving them each a quick hug she picked up the remnant of the roll of duct tape that Deimos had left on the floor and went out of the room. She stood one foot on Grid's back, pulled his wrists together and ran twelve tight wraps of tape around them. His ankles got the same treatment. Just for good measure she zapped him again with the taser, though, by the look of his head wounds, he would not be rising soon, if at all.

"Jordan," she said. "How you doing?"

"Better. I can breathe again, and my eyes are clearing."

Heidi swung open the front door and raised a window to clear the pepper residue, then pulled her phone from a pocket and pressed 911.

"Yes," she said to the phone. "We have Deimos."

Heidi's adrenalin held long enough to force her way, against the wishes of the police and the EMTs, into the ambulance that held Jordan. Deimos was already loaded into another that had driven off with the siren warbling. Jordan lay on the gurney, pain finally showing on his face as his own adrenalin wore off. A technician saw the contorted expression and asked him if he was allergic to any medication. Jordan shook his head and the tech injected a potent, opiate-based pain killer.

Heidi sat, leaning back in exhaustion, eyes closed, but with a hand resting on Jordan's good arm while the techs placed a bandage over his ugly laceration, caused by the flesh pinching between the bone and the club, and isolated the broken arm in an inflatable splint. She had brushed aside police questions at the apartment and insisted that if they could talk to Jordan at the hospital, they could also wait and talk to her there. Rather than delay the repair to Winslow's arm they had let her go with him.

Jordan's shot began to take effect and his face smoothed. He looked at Heidi, the magnificent but spent Heidi. "Are you okay?"

She nodded but he could see that she was ready to succumb to shock. "Hey," he said to the techs, "Heidi's about ready to pass out."

One of them said, "Here, miss. Put your head between your knees and breathe through this mask." She complied and soon became less ashen. She sat back up and smiled weakly through the mask at Jordan. He was ready to smile at the whole world. That was a good shot they'd given him.

A wheel-chair met them at the emergency room entrance and Jordan was transferred to it and rolled inside. Heidi had regained the strength to walk alongside him into the hospital.

Detective Wallace Rasmussen found them in an examination room, awaiting attention for the badly broken arm. "What the hell happened?"

Jordan grinned at him and Heidi shrugged wearily. She said, "Deimos was waiting for us."

"How did he know you'd be there?"

"He knew where I lived before I moved to Jennifer's. He came up behind one of my roommates, Lisa, while she was unlocking the door and forced his way in. He got hold of her from behind with the pipe and threatened to crush her throat if Melanie didn't make the call inviting us over for a party. After we agreed he tied them in the bedroom. When we came in he tried to kill Jordan, but Jord caught the club on his arm and the grocery bag. Then he rushed Deimos and held him until I could get there with the pepper spray and taser. Deimos dropped the club but wouldn't go down, so I picked the pipe up and *made* him go down."

"My magnificent Heidi," Jordan smiled, "saved me. She said 'Let us spray' and God heard her spray and saw that it was good."

"Deimos might die," Rasmussen said, eying Jordan obliquely.

"So what?" Heidi asked.

Rasmussen shook his head. "Even if he lives, the doctors are giving two-to-one odds he won't be mentally competent to stand trial. Brain damage."

Heidi shrugged. Jordan still smiled.

"No clue where he was hiding?"

Heidi shook her head and Jordan fell asleep.

The doctor came in finally to examine the arm but stopped at the crowding in the little room. Rasmussen stood to leave, stopping and turning at the doorway. "When Winslow is sensible again, I need you both to come down to the office for detailed statements."

Heidi nodded.

The doctor deflated the temporary splint, unzipped it and carefully peeled it from the scabbed bandage. He rolled the bandage off, stopping part way to open a gauze to soak up the bleeding. He palpated the arm gently and Jordan woke with a flinch.

"Hey, doc," Jordan grinned.

The doctor nodded to him with a quick smile, scanned Jordan's wrist band into the computer and ordered x-rays.

Another long, dull interval later, Jordan was wheeled off to the x-ray, then returned for another interminable wait, after which they finally rolled him away to a surgery and Heidi was directed to the nearest waiting room. The damage was severe enough that his bones required plates.

After surgery the doctor found Heidi. "The arm was bad, but it should heal okay. We want to keep him overnight and he can check out around ten in the morning. Go home and get some sleep. No offense, but you look terrible. You came with the ambulance, right?" Heidi nodded. "There's a bus-stop half a block down from the emergency room entrance, or, if you want a taxi, just talk to emergency reception. Go down to the end of that hall, turn right and the door there exits to the emergency lobby."

"Thanks," Heidi said blurrily.

She fell deeply asleep when her head hit the pillow, but three hours later she awoke soaked in sweat and nightmare dread. Two hours further along she still lay there listening to the night sounds of Evansville, with visions in her mind of Grid smashing that pipe repeatedly against the backs of Jordan's legs. Heidi got up, tossed off the sweaty, long tee she slept in and slipped across the hall to the bathroom. Hoping it wouldn't wake Jennifer, she got the shower going hot and steamy and stepped in for a long cleansing.

There were clean sheets here somewhere. They turned up in the laundry basket. The damp ones lay crumpled where she threw them in the corner of her room. It felt so good, fresh from the shower, to slip into the crisp clean sheets. But it did not help her sleep.

Around six in the morning she gave up. It's a shame that mirrors don't lie, she thought while looking through that window onto vanity's demise. I look like shit.

She showered again. Say what you might about the impossibility of giving her hair any fashionable style, as long as she kept it short it was a marvel of simple maintenance. Rub it good with the towel, run a hair pick through a few times and it was done.

Not much could be done about the bags under her eyes.

Strangely, Heidi felt a sense of freedom breaking through her exhaustion and through the fear that had not left since the horror in the grove by her apartment. Maybe it was just giddiness from lack of sleep, but maybe it was knowing that the author of the fear was served his just desserts. It would be a nice change to go for a run, which she hadn't done since that night. If she timed it right, she could run over to the hospital and collect Jordan at his release. She'd be sweaty again when she got there, but she didn't give a damn what the staff would think, and Jordan would be doped to the gills. She clipped the spare pepper spray to her waistband as she left.

Jordan was, indeed, doped to the gills, not just for the broken arm and surgery, but to allow him to sit in the wheelchair without agony. The original numbness had passed and his thighs and buttocks ached severely. Heidi collared a taxi to pick them up and maneuvering him into it would have been a feat of slapstick comedy if it hadn't hurt so much.

During the run Heidi had thought about the situation, knowing that Jordan would be non-functional for a time, and that his motel would be intolerable. Jordan, in his vacant state, agreed that it made sense for him to go back to the roomier apartment, so she had the taxi take them to Jordan's old place, waited patiently while he struggled to extract the key from his pants, and then opened the door.

She looked with shock and disgust at the state of the place.

They hobbled into the middle of the living room and looked around with awe. Somebody very angry had spent time here methodically shredding everything. Deimos! Deimos had chosen the one hiding place that nobody considered searching, and had taken out his rage and frustration on Jordan's remaining possessions.

Heidi sighed, noticed the residual stench of unwashed male, and opened the windows, including the one which didn't latch since Deimos had broken it for entry so long ago. At least it seemed long ago. Then, leaving Jordan carefully propped against the wall by the bathroom, she braved the dirty bedroom. She stripped the bed and searched everywhere until she found a couple of clean bath towels. She spread them over the bare mattress and went out to help Jordan creep in and stretch out prone upon them. He looked so vulnerable. Heidi shook her head and sighed again.

Jordan wasn't going anywhere for a while, so she kept his key when she left. The new taxi she had called waited at the curb. Time was at a premium now and it was worth spending a few bucks to get everything done quickly.

Two hours later Jordan's front door opened to the turn of a key and the intent of a driven, sleep deprived woman. She tackled the bedroom first, gently rolling Jordan one way and the other to get him off the towels and onto a sheet. She tossed a cheap new blanket onto him and was reassured by his immediate sleeping breaths.

When she finished, the place looked and smelled as if a person could live there comfortably. Or even two persons. It was obvious that she would have to dress out of her suitcases until she could score a cheap dresser at a thrift store, and the couch did not look very sleepable, but she would manage. She had not discussed these thoughts with Jordan, so it would come as a surprise on waking to realize that he had a roommate.

The surprise was both pleasant and distressing to Jordan. He liked the company, but dreaded the potential for embarrassment, which bore fruit too soon and too deeply.

They shared the worst experience the following day. Late in the afternoon Jordan finally felt an urge to evacuate his bowels despite the paralyzing effect of the pain meds. His legs had become so stiff and sore that he could not stand from the bed without help. Worse, he could not lower himself to the toilet. He tried every conceivable way to manage on his own with one working arm, but there was no option.

"Jord," Heidi said, "we all need help sometimes. And, believe it or not, I have seen men naked."

"Not this man."

"Are you deformed?"

"How would I know? My experience of seeing naked men is limited and fleeting."

"You're worried about comparisons? No, that couldn't be. It's the need for help. It's being a man and having help for a private function."

Jordan frowned through a blush. "Private function. You make it sound like an exclusive dinner party."

"Tell you what. You can tug those briefs down with your good hand while I look away. When you're ready, let me know and I'll reach back to help ease you down."

"Okay."

The bowel-movement took effort and time, and caused much discomfort. He cursed the pain pills and vowed never to use them again. At least he had one good hand to clean himself. But there was no way he could rise on his own; just leaning a bit on the seat awoke the pain demons. The sink was close enough that he could at least wash his hand to guarantee it would be clean when Heidi grabbed it to hoist him. He could contort just enough, biting against the pain, to reach the flush lever. This must be how the elderly feel as they descend to helplessness. After allowing time for the fan to vent the odor he gritted his teeth and called to Heidi for help.

She approached with her head turned aside and pulled him to his feet. He let her hand go and bent as best he could to work his briefs up. When he was ready, she took his good arm and began backing from the room, leading him. The mirror revealed the backs of his legs to her and she gasped. They were horribly discolored with a darker stripe at every pipe blow.

"That bad?" He looked in the mirror, too. "Oh my God!"

He admired the extent and depth of the bruising. Finally, shaking his head he said, "Well, they should heal. Let's go."

He thanked her tersely after he lay on the bed again.

"No," Jord said later when Heidi offered his pill. "Just give me some aspirin. I'm not going through that ordeal again."

She laughed and retreated to find the aspirin.

In three days his legs had limbered enough that he could haul himself up with his good arm, so he no longer had to suffer the indignities of the toilet. A week later he could use the fingers of his left hand for light work, though he still had to rely on Heidi to button his pants. This intimacy, for some reason, was not demeaning, and he shamefully looked forward to it. He was still deep in grief over Catherine, but it did not reduce the speeding of his breath at the touch of the pretty, young Heidi. If she noticed it, she made no sign.

Catherine's father arrived in Evansville on March seventh. He worked quickly through the disposition of his daughter's few possessions. Most of her accumulated wealth lay in the good friends she acquired and the times they had together. This investment involved happy infusions of cash, which left little money to stockpile mundane goods.

After he'd winnowed down to a Volkswagen beetle in the driveway of her rental house, Catherine's father asked among her friends if there was somebody who could best use it. Almost unanimously, they suggested Jordan Winslow, the person most intimate to her at the end and in need of motor transport until he heals up. "Heals up from what?" he asked the first who mentioned it.

This is when he heard how Heidi and Jordan had taken down the fucking bastard that murdered his little girl.

Heidi was at class when the doorbell chimed, but Jordan was mobile again, so he pushed back the chair from the desk where he had been worrying his algorithm. He opened the door to a tall, fit, except for a hint of beer belly, man of about sixty.

"Yes?"

"Hi. I'm Harold Sinjohn, Catherine's father. You're Jordan Winslow?"

"Yes. Very nice to meet you, sir." He extended his hand to shake and invited the man in.

They made small talk while Sinjohn sat at the dining table and Jordan made coffee. When he placed the cups, one at time with his good arm, and sat, Jordan said, "What can I do for you?"

"I hope to do something for you." He glanced at the cast on Jordan's left arm. "I heard about your part in catching Catherine's killer. I wanted to thank you. And Catherine's old car needs a new home. I thought you could use it. Here are the keys and the signed title." He dug into an inside jacket pocket and slid them across the table.

"I-I-I don't know what to say. Thanks. She loved that little car. And I will too. Thank you."

"I think she'd want you to have it. And I want you to have it. You might not know it, but the last two months of her life she changed. Not a lot. She just became....gentler. She talked with relief about getting rid of Tony and finding somebody who proved that some men might not be assholes. That a man could be a partner for life instead of a brief diversion. You made the last weeks of her life worth living. I wish I could give you more than a broken down car."

Jordan had to lower his face. "She was an amazing woman," he said. "I had given up, too, until her."

They sipped at the coffee and gazed, politely ignoring each other's distress, out the window toward the unlit streetlight.

"Well, I have a plane to catch," Sinjohn said, putting down the cup and standing. "Thanks for the coffee. And everything."

Jordan rose with him and followed to the door.

Sinjohn stopped outside and turned. "I wish we'd had a chance to get better acquainted. Good luck."

Jordan nodded. "Thank you, sir." They shook hands and the older man left, pulling a phone from his pocket to call a cab.

"Is that Catherine's VW in the lot?" Heidi asked as she came in the door.

"Not anymore. Her father dropped it off. It's ours now."

"Weird. Providential. Our first rowing competition is on Lake Washington in a week and a half. I thought you'd want to go. And now we have a car."

"Couldn't keep me from it. I'll get the car registered tomorrow and have a mechanic go through it. Catherine had a laissez-faire maintenance philosophy."

They had a brief argument in Seattle as they were checking into the motel. He tried to get two rooms and she insisted that it was a waste of money. One room with two beds was fine. "FerGodsake," she said. "How is it different from your apartment?"

Jordan gave up and shrugged. "Okay," he said turning to the clerk. "One room, two beds."

But he was concerned. His left hand had regained enough strength to button his own pants, clumsily in his cast, so he didn't need Heidi's help for anything anymore. He could manage all the small niceties of life, had taken over the teaching of his dynamics class, and was again attending his own courses. He had even done more than half of the driving to Seattle, using the right knee to help his club-like left hand stabilize the steering wheel while shifting. But he hadn't asked Heidi, or himself for that matter, why she still lived at his place. The embarrassing intimacies they had shared made him want both to push her far away and to keep her as near as possible. The motel argument made him determined to address the question as soon as they returned to Evansville.

The assistant coach gave the crews the old "win one for the Gipper" speech, which would have seemed silly, trite and out-of-line if everybody wasn't already highly amped for the competition and wanting to do their best for their absent coach.

The judges, inspecting State University's boat, decided that the bungee cords had to come out, and that the handicapping weights had to be affixed to the hull and not the rowers' seats. The bow bulge could stay.

"Don't worry," Jordan told the crew. "We thought they wouldn't pass. The real edge we have is in the efficiency of the hull. And your determination."

Catherine had been old fashioned and refused upgrading to an electronic com system, preferring that the cox rely on good lungs and a small megaphone, but had been persuaded that the modern boat deserved modern sound, so the system had been hard-wired into the deck. Some of the engineering students had suggested going wireless, but Winslow and Durning both insisted that hard wiring reduced the risk of interference and increased the reliability. As a backup they installed two identical systems that could be switched in or out by the cox if one failed.

The cox tested both circuits and gave a thumbs-up.

When they were mounting the oars watchers marveled at the odd shape of the blades. A spectator shouted, "Hey, Batwings! You gonna row that thing or fly it?"

The crew grimly ignored the attention and let their flare of anger settle alongside their reservoir of explosive strength. It was like lacing their fuel with nitro-methane.

The boats lunged forward at the start and the cox set the SU team a strong pace to test their opponent. The other craft had timed the start just slightly better and came off the gun with a quarter length lead, but it became obvious in the first thirty yards that, unless they were holding something in reserve, they could not last against SU. The SU boat gained steadily, coming even at a hundred yards. By two hundred they were half a length in front. The cox backed off the pace at a thousand to save the crew and they still crossed the finish line three and a half lengths ahead.

The SU crews, Heidi, Jordan and the support team burst into cheers bigger than their small group seemed capable of generating. They jumped, they whooped, they hugged. If only Coach had been there.

The rest of their matches that weekend went nearly as well. No boat could match their speed, at best finishing only three quarters of a length behind SU. Nobody laughed at the batwings anymore.

It was a euphoric, exhausted team that loaded up that evening for the four hour drive home.

Monday evening Heidi and Jordan sat down after supper for a calculus tutoring session, a practice that had recommenced when Jord could hobble around on his own. They worked through the concepts from her latest classes, then pushed back the books and picked up their nearly empty, cooling teacups.

Neither of them were in a talking mood, and if one caught the other smiling, they knew it was a memory of the glorious rowing competition of the weekend past.

Jordan felt it was time.

"How come you haven't moved back to Jennifer's? You have other friends. You have a life outside. I can manage on my own. Don't get me wrong. I'm glad you're here, I just don't know *why* you're here."

"I'm watching."

He raised his brows. "Watching what?"

"Watching you heal."

He looked at his arm, encased in a bright red, lightweight cast. He wiggled his fingers and looked quizzically at her.

She smiled enigmatically, stood, rinsed the cups at the sink and walked around the breakfast bar, down the hall and into the bathroom.

Heidi baked a two layer, box-mix cake, frosted it in chocolate, and poked thirty-four candles into it to celebrate Jordan's birthday on April second. In a fit of whimsy she stuck many of the candles into the side. She regretted this as soon as she started lighting them.

Their routine settled through the next weeks into comfortable habits with occasional trips to watch their scullers beat every rival. It was almost certain that they would sweep the competition this spring and bring the trophy home, just as Jordan had hoped, and had promised Catherine.

On April twenty-first Heidi came through the door to find an exhilarated Jordan, waiting with two full champagne glasses, one of which he offered to her.

She set her book pack on the floor beside the door and accepted the glass. "What are you glowing about? Why the champagne?"

"I've done it!" he crowed. "My algorithm works!" And he chimed their glasses.

"Congratulations!" she smiled, and stepped into his arms to give a vigorous hug.

He hugged her back with energy, and hugged her with joy, and hugged her with wakening awareness. Long past the time when previous hugs had broken apart, they held to each other while the drinks in their glasses grew warm and flat.

Finally, alarmed, he pushed himself out of her arms. "Whoa," he said. In confusion he clinked his glass to hers again and downed the drink in a gulp.

She made that mysterious smile again and drank her champagne. Jordan vaulted to the refrigerator, extracted the bottle and poured them each a fresh drink.

"Show me," Heidi said, gesturing toward his laptop.

Excited, he walked her through the changes he'd made that day which finally brought his predictions in line with experimental results.

Afterward, they fetched the bottle of sparkling wine and retreated to the couch to finish it. He put his own contentment behind for a moment and asked how her day had been. "Boring," she said.

They got up and put together a simple meal of steamed salmon broken up onto a bed of green salad, with steamed broccoli and baked potatoes. The glow held through supper.

When the meal was eaten, Heidi said, "I'll get dessert."

Jordan watched curiously as she reached in the fridge for the Wensleydale, and pulled Wheat-Thins from the cupboard above. She placed them on the table, sliced a piece of cheese, stacked it onto a cracker, picked it up, reaching across to him, and put it into his mouth.

"Your turn," she said passing the knife to him.

He followed her lead, feeding her a cracker with Wensleydale.

They laughed.

Jordan looked at the clock. "I better clean up." He collected the dishes and started dishwater running. While the sink filled he put away the food. He whistled Simon and Garfunkel's '59th Street Bridge Song'.

She watched him a while. "I need a shower."

"Okay," he said over his shoulder. "Then we can watch 'Antiques Roadshow' before bed."

She came in as he was stacking the last item in the drying rack. She turned on the TV, pulled her robe tightly around herself and sat on the couch. He joined her.

At the end of the show, Jordan shut off the TV and stood to stretch. "Been a good day. Sleep well."

Heidi went to the closet where she stored her bedding through the day. She pulled her pillow out. She checked the entry door lock. She walked around the front rooms turning out lights and then followed Jord into the bedroom.

Jordan was sitting on the edge of his bed removing his shoes when she came through the door. He watched her with astonishment as she walked to the other side of the bed, tossed her pillow onto the head end, removed her robe and stood in her long-tee nightshirt. He noticed that somehow she had transformed from the seven he had originally rated her to a perfect ten.

"You've healed," she said.

On May tenth Jordan pulled onto the street distractedly, narrowly missed by an outraged, honking Toyota. He cursed himself aloud in the privacy of the car and mused that he had been much too distracted for much too long. Was this what life would be about in the future? Would he float along battered around by the currents of chance and the whims of people he had never met? Of course that's exactly how it would be, just as it always had been despite the conviction that he was steering his own course. What more proof did he need than his long ago, disastrous marriage to Satan's Sister?

He had an appointment in twenty minutes with his college dean regarding unethical behavior that, as stipulated in his TA contract, could result in censure and possible removal from his post. The specified unethical behavior was his cohabitation with a student. It was odd that, until his cast was removed, nobody seemed to think it unusual that his live-in caretaker happened to be a pretty, young student, as if his disabled arm either exempted them from usual rules, or interfered with amoral activities. Both ideas were ridiculous, so the summons to appear before the dean at this late moment was equally ridiculous.

Jordan's assessment of Heidi's sheltered, innocent character had taken an abrupt turnaround on the night she followed him to bed. She was sweet and vulnerable, but she was not reserved, nor unpracticed. Still, she maintained a delightfully fresh, eager, exploratory approach to physical love. If her rape caused any residual issue with intimacies, it was not apparent.

He had severe reservations about the giant step they had taken, but Heidi made it very clear that any coercion she suffered had nothing to do with his position as authority figure, and everything to do with her respect and love for him. They had shared unimaginable stresses, and found only strength and generosity in each other. If that wasn't a basis for love, what could be? They both still felt the sharp grief of Catherine's loss, leavened with guilt at their coupling so soon after her death, but love and time are the remedy for grief. They each committed themselves without remark to that time. Whenever Jordan was overtaken by sadness and retreated inward she left him alone unless it went too long, then she would straddle his lap, press her forehead against his and ask, "Are you there?" He would come out slowly, smile and kiss her. They would cuddle then on the couch in a fading melancholia. Later their lovemaking was especially gentle.

At breakfast after their first night together, between glowing smiles and spontaneously erupting laughter, Jordan had brought up their age difference.

Heidi said, "Grandfather was fifteen years older than Grandmother. She still loves him and he's been dead for twenty years. You only have fourteen years on me. If it bothers you, just call it a family tradition."

Even if he could communicate all of this to the dean, would it be pertinent? The dean knew the horrible events of the past months, but not in detail. Given those details, would he see that nothing could be unethical about Jordan's relationship with Heidi? Would he see that school ethics were vanishingly insignificant beside these events?

"The least perception of scandal. That's the problem," dean Montaigne said. "I don't care that you are genuinely in love, that you shared horrors nobody should suffer, that she's a legal adult or that she's not in your class anymore. The facts are that she *was* in your class, she passed with the highest grade in the class, you're a man, she's a girl, and now you're taking payment for that grade."

Jordan tried to speak but the dean held up his hand. "Or *perceived* to be taking payment. That's the issue. Not what is, but what seems. If I don't fire you, parents will be pounding on my door. Speaking of which, I have notified Ms van Vleet's family of your pending dismissal. To put ..."

"You WHAT?"

"To put the lid back on the kettle before it spills over."

"We were going to tell them at the end of term. You shouldn't have done that."

"Mr. Winslow, I'm sorry if your personal life takes a back seat to the good of the university, but I'm a college dean. You can see my side."

"Sure. The side of a man who ... Never mind. How does this affect my master's program?"

"It doesn't. The university has no interest in the relationships of adult students."

"So I just have to come up with the extra money myself."

The dean shrugged, then nodded.

Jordan had enough in savings to get through to the end of term, but he wouldn't have quite enough for the fall semester to collect the rest of the classwork credits he needed for the masters degree. He might have to delay his studies until he could find a job, preferably here in Evansville and with flex-hours to fit a class schedule.

There was a plus side of course. Losing his TA duties freed more time to refine his algorithm and begin writing his thesis. And only two weeks of school remained.

"Your parents..." Jordan started to say.

"Just called me," Heidi said. "They demanded to know what the hell has been going on. I gave them an edited version. They're not happy."

"I'm sorry. That bastard dean had no right." After a pause he asked, "How edited?"

"They don't know about my first encounter with Deimos. Either our dean didn't say, or didn't know. And I gave you full credit for taking Deimos down. I didn't want them to think I was that close to trouble." She smiled. "And maybe being my shining knight will help them over the age difference."

"I thought it was a family tradition."

"Not so much when it skips a generation."

On May 12 they attended a sculling competition at Riverbend Park. Their teams swept the field, or river, in good style. Heidi noticed a competing coach chatting with State University's acting coach, Beth, who looked around until she spotted Jordan and pointed him out. Heidi nudged Jordan and said, "Somebody looking for you."

The approaching woman was mid-forties, with a black skullcap of hair, tall like all rowers who became coaches, of Asian ancestry with a wide face and small nose. "You're Jordan Winslow?" she asked.

Jordan nodded, reaching out a hand to shake.

"I'm Madelaine Wu, coach for Midland U. I understand you designed and built that killer shell for State."

Jordan smiled but resisted the urge to call her a walking poem. "I helped direct the project."

"We have the funds to upgrade. I want you to make one for us."

Jordan's eyebrows jumped. "I don't have a facility. It was a school lab project."

"Would you develop the facility? We want to be first on your list. If we can get one of those boats..." She smiled and shrugged.

Heidi nudged him and, when he glanced at her, gave him a nod and head gesture toward the coach.

Here it was, another of those random forces that direct a life-path, and, like those he'd faced before, there was no hint of outcome. Would this path lead to joy or disaster?

He said. "How do I contact you?"

She pulled her phone out and displayed the number. He punched it into his.

As soon as Ms Wu was out of hearing range Heidi said, "Jord! This is it. This is how you fund your degree!"

He looked skeptical. "We can think about it. But there are serious problems."

"My dad says problems are just opportunities in disguise."

"What kind? Spy disguise? Inspector Clouseau disguise?"

She punched him.

That evening at supper they discussed it.

Jordan said, "I don't have the money to build a mold, buy the materials, rent a building, install the air filters, vents, and the oven, hire the people. It can't work."

"Come on. There has to be a way. Borrow the money? Get an advance?"

Jordan thought. "Credit's too tight. Maybe the advance. I'll call Wu tomorrow and see if she's that desperate. But we don't even know what it costs to build a shell. Definitely don't know what to charge for one."

"Ask the college. They built the first one. There must be a record."

Jordan leaned across the table, pulled her face to his and kissed her. "You are a genius."

"I thought you already knew that." She smiled.

The next morning he called Wu, got her voice mail, and left a message asking if she could forward fifty percent of the cost to help prime the pump. He stopped by Professor Durning's office.

Durning did not like Winslow. This had never been in question. But the professor was a rational, if self-interested, man. His knee-jerk reflex at Jordan's query was to deny access to the college data. The idiot had been fired for immorality, for God's sake. What right did he have to any of the records? But when it became clear that the goal was production and sale of the boat that the lab had created, his better side overrode the enmity. Or at least his pecuniary side spoke up.

"Tell you what," Durning said. "I'll let you have the cost spreadsheet. But it'll be useless to you. Ask me why."

Jordan, barely controlling his urge to stand and walk away, said, "Why."

"Because," Durning smirked, "The university patents everything that comes out of the labs. The application for the racing shell is already filed. Use it if you want to face a lawsuit."

Jordan stood and stepped toward the door.

"Wait. You'll want to hear the rest." Jordan gritted his teeth, stopped and turned. Durning continued, "First, all of the contributors, including me and you, have their names on the application. Read your contract. Second, the university is willing to license the patent."

Winslow's phone hummed. He pulled it out and read the text from Wu. "What cost fifty per?"

He slowly pocketed the phone. "Okay," he said. "Who do I have to see to start the wheels?"

"Try university admin."

"Okay. I'll call you."

Durning's contract with the university was not like Jordan's. Durning was a full professor and had a small paragraph which granted him a mite of the license fee for any commercial use of patents in which he was a contributor. A TA got bragging rights and that was all.

Jordan paused in the hall outside of Durning's office and texted back to Wu, "TBA. Wait."

There was no problem with licensing the rights, no problem getting the data from Durning, and no problem dreaming of the completed racing shell, but the money would still be a big problem. Heidi and Jordan sat at the dining table working through the spreadsheet, adding costs and factoring in the time students put into actual construction. They assumed a living wage for anybody replicating the boat commercially. The sum was a very large number. And they had not yet included the prorated fronting cost of the facility, overhead and incidentals.

"I hate to be redundant," Heidi said. "But maybe you should talk to the college again."

"About?"

"Buying the mold, the bag and the oven." At his smile she asked, "Do I get another kiss?"

He stood, took her hand, lifted her out of the chair and led her toward the bedroom. Prices for good ideas were rising, as well as other things.

Jordan, following Heidi's line of thought further, contacted the students from the lab to see if they were interested in repeating the work, but for pay this time. Three who didn't have other plans for the summer said yes.

No other cost-saving shortcuts popped up. It came down to either paupering himself by maxing out his credit cards or looking for venture capital. He considered the added responsibility of tying his fate, for good or ill, to Heidi, and decided to look around for outside capital to cut his own risk. This led him as a first choice, reluctantly, to consider his brother, Walter Winslow II.

His brother, five years older, and he were not close. The elder son was named for their father and, by all tradition, should have been called Walt Junior, but he was so weirdly pleased by the abbreviation of his name to "WW II" that he used *the second*, instead. Walter had taken a career path, if it could be called that, completely different from Jordan. He attended one year of college and dropped out to go to Mexico for over a year of hazily described occupations. Upon Walt's return home

Jordan admired his brother's marvelously tanned hide and the two inch scar just below his hairline at the left temple. He wouldn't talk about the scar and nobody asked about the tan. Following his very brief stop with the family Walt had boarded the bus to Las Vegas and taken a job dealing black-jack. Before the real estate boom really picked up speed Walt and his roommates overextended their credit and bought a house on spec. They flipped it for a handsome profit and bought two more. Walt built on his paper wealth until, in 2006, Jordan visited him and said, "You're kidding. No property in the desert is worth that." Walt and his partners sold all of their holdings, Walt put his money in certificates-of-deposit, lived briefly in Los Angeles, returned without explanation to his childhood home town of Flagstaff, and rented an apartment in apparent retirement. He had accumulated several million dollars that did not go down the toilet when real estate crashed. As the interest paid on CDs dropped he started looking for small venture-capital investments. Occasionally he called Jordan for a slant on technology offerings and found that the advice unerringly added to his wealth. By the time Jordan lost his job at Boeing, his brother's worth cracked a hundred million dollars.

Jord thought his brother might feel an obligation. It was worth a try.

"Yes," Jord said to the phone. "Purely venture. No guarantee. Running through the numbers, it should pay off in two years if we sell twelve boats a year."

"And that's likely?"

"If the teams want to stay in competition."

"Okay. I'm in. How much?"

Jordan tensed his muscles and said, "Two hundred thousand."

"Great. Where do I send it?"

Jordan thought he could learn to love his black-sheep, wealthy brother.

The money popped into the new business account three days later. Jordan and Heidi couldn't help themselves; they celebrated themselves sick. During the revelry they laughingly decided an appropriate company name must be had immediately. "Shells R Us" didn't even get a groan. "Long and Wet" was inappropriate and obviously stemmed from other intruding thoughts. "Shell-Edge" kept their interest long enough to be considered final, at least for their drunken brainstorming.

"I really love it when you ply me with illegal drink," Heidi breathed.

"You're twenty."

"But not twenty-one."

"Mmm, that's hot."

She ground against him. "I can tell."

At twelve minutes after ten the next morning they quietly, regretfully, nursed their black coffees. A knock pounded at the front door and into their throbbing heads. They looked at each other, waiting for one to volunteer, shrugged and stood together to face the unwelcome intrusion.

A very polite man stood there asking, "Are you Heidi van Vleet and..." he glanced at an envelope in his hand. "Jordan Winslow?"

They nodded.

"Great," he said holding the two envelopes out toward them. Even sober people, a group foreign to them at the moment, automatically accept an offered object. It has something to do with primordial hominid behavior. So they took them, and the polite man smilingly hurried away.

"You are hereby summoned..." the papers began.

Gerard Deimos, his family, et al, required their depositions preliminary to the three million dollar civil suit they were bringing against Heidi and Jordan for the assault and severe bodily injury upon the beloved son, Gerard.

Jordan dug through his wallet and found the worn card of Roger Menken, esq., the attorney James had found for him when accused of Catherine's murder. He called Menken and they settled on a retainer to get through the depositions with an understanding that a trial would require additional fees. They scheduled a meeting to discuss testimony.

"My best advice," Menken said after hearing the story, "is to tell it just like you told me, and then answer all the questions honestly. You both claim self-defense and the women illegally restrained in the bedroom support that. Nothing either of you did can allow a claim."

"You don't think Deimos can milk sympathy from a jury? He's still in a nursing home, unfit for trial. Barely able to speak or walk."

"We'll petition for hearing by a judge. A judge will have all the facts at hand and be less influenced by a pitiable image."

They spent their spare time that week looking at buildings to house the boat factory, and securing sources for the materials that they would need. They incorporated Shell-Edge LLC, listing James, Dave, and Jennifer as corporate officers, along with themselves.

They would have barely noticed the ending of term if not for the strident demands of Heidi's parents to explain, again, what the hell was going on. She had not used the plane ticket home. An angry call from her father left her in tears that Jordan could not console. A breach between them was devastating to poor Heidi. He had taught her more than just how to play chess. He was the rock to which her life's foundation was bound. But she stuck to her decision and did not go home.

Sculls racing would continue for six weeks and the next meet brought them two more prospective clients. The three new employees broke down the equipment they had built in the lab and transported it to the defunct roller rink that Heidi and Jordan had leased.

Heidi and Jordan returned home exhausted after six hours of depositions. Menken had encouraged them with smiles and nods but never interrupted the process no matter how far afield the questions wandered. The query rambled into their upbringing as children, family history, and high-school grades, then jumped back to another repetition of the incident at question, Gerard's victimization. The story had to be told over and over again, front to back, back to front, from the imagined perspective of the women in the bedroom, what Jordan assumed Heidi was experiencing and vice-versa, exploring emotions, counting seconds, counting blows.

The Deimos attorney, to his chagrin, while exploring previous acquaintanceship stumbled onto the news of Heidi's alleged beating and rape by Gerard. Between now and the trial he would have to figure out whether this nugget could be of use to him or was better left alone.

The process seemed arbitrary and pointless to Jordan and Heidi, but Menken was accustomed to the ritual and detected intent in the pattern. "They only have one point to anchor their suit. They're going to claim excessive use of force. Self defense in this state only excuses you to the point of insuring your own safety. Any injury, or death, beyond that leaves you liable. But I think they'll have a hard time convincing the judge."

"Dad!" Heidi cried with delight and trepidation. "What are you doing here?"

Desmond van Vleet stood glowering in the apartment doorway but did not move. Heidi's face crumpled. Her father softened and he said, "Shush, shush." He would have hugged her except they had barely touched since she turned twelve. "Shush. Can I come in?"

She wiped her tear darkened eyes, backed and waited for him to enter. He came in looking around and sniffing the air. His face crinkled with distaste at the imagined scent of the inappropriately older man living in this place with his daughter. A father always must come to terms with losing his child to another man, but this whole situation was outrageous. The newspaper articles and rumors about this place, this man, and his little girl, suggested terrible things. His eventual acquiescence did not extend to sacrificing his daughter to ill luck and her own bad judgment.

"So, where's this Whimsy guy?"

"Winslow. Jordan. He's either at the engineering library working on his master's thesis, or at the factory he's building on the strength of his own character ..."

"Okay, okay. So he's God's gift to ambitious entrepreneurs, but I need to meet him."

"Dad, you'll like him."

"For Godsake, Hy. What do you expect? You've been in the middle of a load of crap for a long time and lied about it. You think I'm going to feel good about this guy?"

"If you knew him ..."

The front door opened. Jordan came in with the usual smile at coming home to his Heidi, but froze at the unexpected scene. Heidi had been crying and his first desire was to kick this guy in the head, but understanding restrained the impulse as family features common to the pair became apparent. It was her father. Oh, God, he thought. Not good.

"Mr. Van Vleet?" he asked going forward with outstretched hand.

"Mr. Whim... Winslow."

They shook hands and the room became uncomfortably quiet.

Heidi blurted, "I'll make tea!"

"Heidi told us that you saved her from the man that killed her coach, but I checked the newspaper archive and they say it was the other way around."

"It was a ..."

"He did save me, Dad," she called from the kitchen. "If he hadn't taken that first hit, I would be dead."

"You said you were never in danger."

"Well, look how upset you are now. I didn't want you and Mom to worry."

Van Vleet shook his head. "Kids," he muttered. He looked at Jordan. "And you're what, thirty, thirty-one?"

"Thirty-four."

"God. Well, I'm not supposed to raise a stink about that. My mother takes her granddaughter's side and threatened to disown me. You two getting married?"

"Dad!"

"Okay, okay. Twenty-first century. I know. Sorry to be direct, Winslow, but it sounds like Hy has had a rough time and kept it from us. We're her *family* and she won't come to us for help. She knows she can tell us anything."

Heidi walked into the room with the teapot and three cups. Jordan looked at her with raised brows and nodded subtly toward her father. He looked back at van Vleet and asked, "Anything?"

The man's attention sharpened and he gave Heidi an edged look. She kept her gaze down while she set the table and said, "There is one more thing. The thing that started it all." She sat down beside Jordan as close as possible to him without actually touching and finally looked at her father. "The man that killed Coach, the man that Jordan and I put in the hospital, beat and raped me last fall."

Her father's jaw dropped. "God damn it! Why didn't you ..." He saw that it had taken all of her nerve, and the presence of this Jordan guy to tell him this, and, still, she was ready to run from the room at the first wrong word, which he might already have said. But she didn't run. A tear leaked from each eye.

Jordan watched her tenderly for a moment, then took her hand.

"Good God," van Vleet said quietly. "You could have told us. We would have helped you through it."

"No," she said. "You would have been like everybody else and told me to report it. But until it happens to you, you have no idea how hard that is." She squeezed Jordan's hand, turned and smiled at him. "Jordan never pushed me. He offered a strong shoulder, but treated me like a normal person. That's what I needed at the time, and part of why I fell in love with him."

142

Van Vleet struggled with his own emotions. "I guess I understand. I wish you had let us in, but," he glanced briefly at Jordan, "Apparently you had it handled. That's part of growing up, and I never doubted that you would be a survivor. Mr. Winslow, Jordan, I suppose I seem a real ass, barging into your home with an attitude. But we never knew the whole story. What were we supposed to think?"

Jordan said, "You haven't done anything I wouldn't. Believe me, I want to protect your daughter too."

Van Vleet nodded and looked at the pot in the center of the table. "Is that tea steeped yet?"

Heidi smiled and poured.

Before his flight out the next morning Heidi's father took them to breakfast. There he learned about the civil suit and cursed the idiocy of the world. When he parted privately with his daughter outside airport security, he said, "You were right. I like Jordan. You fit each other. Good luck, but, please keep us informed. We're adults. We can take it. Maybe a little panic and overreacting at first, but we can take it. And bring him to meet your mother when you can. Nothing I tell her will put her at ease."

The electrical panel at the roller rink was barely adequate to the needs of the factory. Their piecemeal oven design was the saving grace. The multiple elements were split off to different breakers to spread the load. It was marginal, but legal, and it worked. It was a shame to install new, state-of-the-art air filtration next to the salvage-built oven, but practicality and economy overrode aesthetics.

Jordan called Madelaine Wu with the figure they needed for the fifty percent down. She did not gasp, so he feared that they were underpricing their product. "Send the contract," Wu said, "And I'll get it signed and sent back with the check."

Suspecting that they would overextend their capacity, but gripped by the hunger of a new entrepreneur, Jordan contacted the other two potential clients and got them to commit to the half down and a fall delivery on their shells.

Two competitions were left in the sculling season. When State U won the first, Jordan added two more prospective buyers to his list.

Heidi kept glancing at Jordan. Before they left the apartment she said, "I had no idea you would look that good in a suit. Makes me want to tear it off and commit pleasurable acts upon your body."

"And you look *hot* dressed up. But we have to get to the courthouse."

The trial went the way Menken had predicted until the plaintiff's lawyer, Critchfield, was questioning Heidi and became more aggressive.

"Ms van Vleet, in describing the struggle, both you and Mr. Winslow have stated that Mr. Deimos had been forced against the wall by Mr. Winslow. Is this correct?"

"Yes."

"At which time you disabled him with pepper spray?"

"No."

"What? Shall I have the transcript read?"

"Sure, if you want. But what I said was that I sprayed him. He was not disabled."

"How did you conclude that?"

144

"By the beating he was giving Mr. Winslow's buttocks and legs with the pipe."

The gallery chuckled.

Critchfield continued, "So, you then attacked Mr. Deimos with a contact taser?"

"Yes."

"At which point he dropped the pipe?"

"Yes."

"What did you do then?"

"I pulled Mr. Winslow away."

"What did Mr. Deimos do?"

"Nothing. He just stood there."

"Was he disabled at that time?"

"No."

"Why did you conclude that?"

"Because he was still standing."

"Was he leaning against the wall?"

"I guess."

"That's where Mr. Winslow had pushed him. Was he still leaning against the wall?"

"Yes, probably, everything was happening very fast, I don't remember absolutely."

"But you assumed from his upright posture that he was not disabled?"

"That's right."

"How about subdued?" Critchfield asked.

"What do you mean?"

"Incapacitated enough to pose no threat while you called for the police. He had been pepper sprayed and tased. Surely he was in no condition to continue the assault."

"No. Not disabled. Not subdued. It's a small apartment. What could I have done if he'd come after me again? Like you said, it was a contact taser. You have to be in arm's reach, and his arms are longer than mine."

"But he was just standing, right?"

"Yes."

"What did you do?"

"I picked up the weapon he'd tried to kill us with and hit him until he fell."

"Have you considered that he must have been disabled by the taser or he wouldn't have dropped the pipe?"

"Yes, and I rejected that reasoning. A jolt from a taser can cause involuntary muscle contractions during application but won't permanently paralyze a person."

"Are you a taser expert?"

"I read the instructions."

The gallery chuckled again.

Critchfield frowned.

Previous testimony had varied on the number of strikes she made with the pipe before Deimos fell. The hysterical women taped together in the bedroom couldn't agree. Jordan was adamant that it was four, but he was blinded by pepper spray and in severe pain from his own injuries.

"Are you sure that you didn't strike him twice before he fell and twice after?"

"Yes," Heidi said.

"You said three times in your deposition."

She looked puzzled. "No I didn't."

He handed her a bit of the transcript. "Read this."

She read, "I hit him three or four times and he finally fell."

The lawyer took the page back and re-read it with emphasis on "three".

"Can you state with absolute confidence that you did NOT strike the fourth blow when Mr. Deimos was already on the floor and no longer a threat?"

"Yes."

The lawyer turned to the judge. "Your Honor, the defendant is disingenuous. She was in a highly agitated state, but enough in control to wash the pepper spray from her boyfriend's ..."

Menken interrupted. "They were not romantically linked at that time."

"Okay. She had the wherewithal to get Mr. Winslow's eyes washed, and to release her former roommates. She knew exactly what she was doing. She struck Mr. Deimos three times. He fell. She hit him again when he lay helpless. Pure excess. She stepped over the line from self defense to vigilantism. In hindsight she realizes she stepped over that line and is twisting her story to obscure that fact."

He sat down, nodded to Menken and said, "Your questions."

Menken asked Heidi, "How many times did you strike Gerard Deimos before he fell?"

"Four."

"Did you hit him after he fell?"

"No."

"No more questions," Menken said and sat down.

Because it was a civil suit and did not include a jury, the process moved quickly. The plaintiff's arguments were finished by lunch, and the defense began at two o'clock.

Jordan was called back to the stand. Menken asked him to describe, again, what he had sensed—the sound of four blows, the thunder of the Deimos fall, the hazy view of Heidi ready to keep Deimos down with another strike if he tried to rise, his own call for assistance.

Menken thanked Jordan and turned him over to Critchfield.

"Was your arm broken?"

"Yes."

"Did it hurt?"

"I suppose. I was in a state of shock."

"So, you were in shock and blinded by pepper spray."

"I'd only got a spatter of it because my face was turned away."

"Could you see when Ms van Vleet hit Mr. Deimos with the pipe?"

"No, but shortly after he fell."

"You were in shock and blind when she actually struck the blows?"

"Yes."

"No more questions."

Free Body Diagram

Menken asked Dr. Tornsen to appear as witness. He handed a folder to the Judge and said, "The doctor is an expert in blunt force trauma to the human skull. His credentials are given in this file. Will you question his expertise, your honor?"

The judge looked at the papers in the folder. "No. I've seen these before. Would Mr. Critchfield like to question the expert witness?"

"No. I am familiar with his bona fides."

Menken began, "Dr. Tornsen, assuming that the type of injury and the weapon are as described in testimony, can you tell at which angle the weapon was aligned when it struck?"

"Yes."

"Is there any variation in that angle?"

"No. Except that three blows were to the left of the skull and one to the right."

"You mean, even though three were to one side and one blow to the other, no other change in angle is indicated."

"Yes."

"If one of these blows was delivered while both assailant and assaulted were standing, and another while the assailant was standing and the assaulted was lying face down on the floor, could you tell the difference?"

"Yes."

"Was there any difference in the angle of the blows that would indicate the change from standing to prone?"

"No."

"Thank you. That's all we have."

Critchfield asked the only questions he could think of that might distract from the point. "Can you tell in which order the blows were struck?"

"Yes, if the damage overlaps."

"Can you tell if a blow was struck from in front of the victim or behind?"

"Yes."

"How?"

"Contact occurs first at a point nearer the assailant. The rebound at that point causes the hands of the attacker to slow and the skull to accelerate, allowing the faster moving tip of the weapon to roll the far end of contact in against the skull. The tissue damage and the type of fracture at initial contact are different from the far end at last contact."

Critchfield considered the value of the answer to his next question. If the answer was yes, he had a chance to argue further. If no, he was harming his own case. He decided to take the risk. "Was there any change in orientation of the attack from front to back, or back to front?"

"No."

"That's all," Critchfield said, disappointed.

Menken asked, "Were the blows delivered from front or back?"

"All four were delivered from the front."

"Thank you. No more questions."

The judge asked if there was any other evidence or testimony. Both attorneys said, "No."

"In that case I will consider the evidence and render a judgment one week from today. This hearing is adjourned."

Free Body Diagram

"All rise," the bailiff called and the trial was done.

Jord and Heidi were so tense after the trial that they just shed their fancy clothes, poured two glasses of wine and reclined in their underwear together on the couch, looking out at the ubiquitous streetlight, now quenched by the late afternoon sunlight.

A quiet hour passed. Jordan said, "I don't know whether to cut that damned thing down or install a plaque on it."

"What. The streetlight? The wine really hit you, didn't it."

"Just planning for the future."

"Odd kind of future that makes you want to attack a harmless lamppost."

"It's just seen too much. Watching us through that window all the time. It has to either be destroyed or welcomed into the family."

"Weird mood. You okay?"

"Probably. Just overwhelmed at the pace of life. It would be nice to get off the galloping horse sometimes and just walk. We've been through three lifetimes worth of crap in the last eight months."

"I wish I could promise it'll change. I want it to. But we still have what got us through all of that crap: Each other. I think it's going to be okay even if it's hell."

He squeezed her and kissed her nose. "You are a marvel," he said. "Your dad is right. You're a survivor."

The factory was complete and checked, and supplies had arrived. Jordan and Heidi joined the new employees to begin laying-up the first hull in the mold. The inexperience made work slow, but they had time and they were all bright, creative people.

They worked hard each day until the next court date, and this was good because work distracted from the impending doom. If the case went against them, they would lose everything that they had just built. There would be no reason to create a profitable corporation if all the effort would go to paying off the outrageous suit.

The judge entered and everyone rose. "Are the interested parties here?" he asked.

"Yes, your honor," both attorneys chimed.

"Fine. The central claim by plaintiffs, that one of the defendants hit the attacker, Gerard Deimos, after he was incapacitated, has not been established. The expert witness testified that the blows to Deimos' head had all clearly been delivered with the relative positions of the antagonists unchanged and from the front, standing. The suggestion by plaintiffs, that Mr. Deimos was already disabled though he remained upright, is insupportable. The defendant is certainly justified in assuming that he still presented an undiminished threat. Great weight must be given to the perspective of the defendant. Intent plays a major role. If she reasonably believes that she is in imminent peril then her actions are defensive. Mr. Deimos was in the apartment for the purpose of causing bodily harm or murder upon the persons of Ms van Vleet and Mr. Winslow. He attacked them without provocation. Ms van Vleet knew that the police were seeking Mr. Deimos on a warrant of murder, and in fact had been warned by the police to minimize public activities to reduce her own risk from him. For her to assume anything except an ongoing threat from the man while he still stood would be irrational. And the law allows deadly force in the protection of others. Mr. Winslow was also in jeopardy. Finally, she had no assurance that her roommates had not already been murdered.

"I find for the defendants. Court is adjourned."

The ongoing medical assessment of Grid Deimos deemed that he would never be fit to stand trial for the murder of Catherine Sinjohn. He had deteriorated from a mass of trained muscle to a lump of pale, doughy fat. He would never again speak or walk without difficulty, nor could he ever threaten another person; the club strikes to his skull had essentially lobotomized him.

After the unsuccessful suit that his family had pursued, Grid was transported to an institution near his parents' home and disappeared from society, if not from the memories of those he had harmed.

Heidi took a break from the factory work to design business cards and, after appreciative approval from Jordan, submit them for printing. The employees and Jordan released the hull and deck from their molds and began the trimming and finish work before adding bulkheads and joining the parts into a unit.

The boat was not done yet by the final competition of the season, but Jordan, Heidi and the factory bunch were all there to cheer the State University teams and to hand out business cards to anyone who would hold still long enough to hear the remark, "We built SU's shell and are now in production for the commercial market."

Most of the recipients glanced at the remarkable craft that had swept the season so far, accepted the card and slipped it into a wallet or pocket.

SU won in a series of tight races and claimed the trophy.

Two weeks later Jordan called Madelaine Wu to pick up her finished boat and pay the remaining money. When Wu drove off with their creation safely cradled in the trailer, Jordan said, "Gather 'round, troops."

He led them to the lunchroom, pulled the champagne bottle from the refrigerator and, again, contributed to the corruption of youth. He thanked them all repeatedly and told them to take the rest of the week off. "We'll see you Monday and start the next shell. Have a good weekend."

When they were alone he turned to Heidi. "As for you," he said, "come with me."

"Where to?" she asked when he turned the Volkswagen away from, not toward, home. She realized that she had misread the mischievous sparkle in his eye.

"You'll see."

On the outskirts of town he turned into the gravel parking lot of an old, windowless, block building. A sign on the wall read "Dancing Wednesdays. $5.00 per person."

"What's this?" Heidi asked.

"It's called swing, it's fun, and it's great exercise."

www.ingramcontent.com/pod-product-compliance
Lightning Source LLC
Chambersburg PA
CBHW030516260626
47157CB00005B/1767